The Road To Beyond

Micki Pagano

Published by Branding Shorts Books, 2022.

This is a work of fiction. Similarities to real people, places, or events are entirely coincidental.

THE ROAD TO BEYOND

First edition. September 9, 2022.

Copyright © 2022 Micki Pagano.

ISBN: 979-8215752609

Written by Micki Pagano.

For those who grieve. And those who hope.

"There is no reality except the one contained within us."

- Hermann Hesse

CHAPTER 1

SHE WOKE UP UNDER A BRIGHT BLUE SKY. YET, IT WAS snowing. She sat up, brushed the white flecks from her face, and discovered that they were not snowflakes. They were tiny bits of paper floating down like confetti from a cloudless sky. Where was it coming from? The day was like a summer breeze. She inhaled its sweetness. It felt familiar. But why?

The flurry of paper snow subsided. The last of the tiny white bits melted into the concrete ground like shaved ice on a scorching summer day. But it wasn't hot at all. The temperature was just perfect. She looked around. The sidewalk was endless. There was nothing on the horizon. Nothing. No street, no grass, no dirt. Just pavement.

Where was she? Who was she?

Her heart raced.

What happened to her?

"Hello?"

Her small voice rang hollow in the silence.

Stay calm, she said to herself. She knew it was the only way she could find answers. She took a deep breath and stood up. Dust covered her black dress pants and sleeveless turtleneck. She brushed off her clothes. What was this dust?

She looked around again. Every direction was the same. North, East, South, and West. Blue sky. Endless sidewalk.

How old was she? What did she look like? She looked at her hands. Young and groomed, manicured and clean. Her palms held a web of intricate lines, erratic, short and broken. The roadways of her destiny. Her hands spoke. If only she could decipher the language. They held knowledge she so desperately needed.

She closed her hands and looked at the sky. The sun seared the blue. The sounds of her breathing broke the silence.

Was she dreaming?

If this were a dream, she'd wake up soon. Dreams didn't last that long. This morsel of knowledge gave her comfort. Strange, she thought, an odd collection of memories lingered. Though she couldn't remember her name, she did remember trivial nonsense, recollections she wished she could put to better use. Perhaps it was part of a collective consciousness. Why could she remember random things but couldn't recall one detail about yesterday?

She sighed and looked around again. What should she to do next? A song came to mind. She began humming it until the words tumbled out.

"Happy birthday to you..." She sang though she didn't know whose birthday it was. The song was her companion. It filled the silence with hope. Maybe, eventually, she would remember other things too.

"Happy birthday, dear you, happy birthday to you..."

She picked a direction and walked.

IN THE DISTANCE, A stream of purple smoke formed a giant Cumulous cloud on the horizon.

She trotted closer and stopped. What if this meant danger? The plume was thick and dense. What if was a clue? She had to find out.

She was close enough now to see it. A man was swatting the ground with his black coat. His white shirt was stained. Blue suspenders held up thick charcoal pants. He coughed.

He looked up, startled.

"Who are you?"

"Who are you?" she asked in turn.

"If you're just here to confuse me more, get out," he yelled.

"Confusing you? I'm sorry, but who are you?" she asked.

He examined her face, body and gestures, suspicious.

"What's your name?" He coughed again. Soot covered his face, hands and clothes as if he had just emerged from a fire.

His red-rimmed eyes were soulful, deep, yet filled with fear. Was he was afraid of her?

"I don't know who I am," she whispered.

He looked at her, then at the splattered dark area on the concrete. He touched the charred cement and sampled the black embers between his fingertips.

"Did you see it too?"

"I saw the smoke. I followed the smoke here."

He nodded, then looked at her, wondering if he could trust her.

"You didn't see her then."

"Who?"

"Her. The woman with scarves."

"No. I saw no one but you."

The man was quiet. He seemed shaken but didn't want to admit it. Was he crazy? Was she in danger? Could she trust this stranger?

"What's your name?" she asked.

The man stood up, brushed the embers from his hands, and said, "I don't know."

She felt a kinship. Why were they both in the same predicament? She noticed his feet. "No shoes either?"

He looked down and wiggled the toes.

"Look, me too," she said. "I don't know how I got here."

"You don't?"

"I just woke up and started to walk. That's when I found you."

He sighed, relieved. "Me too. I don't remember anything either."

The smoke was gone from the sky.

"What happened?"

"I'm not sure." He paused. "I feel like I survived something. I can't explain."

"Oh. Are you a fireman?"

"A fireman?" He noticed his clothing.

"You look like a fireman, the way you're dressed. And, you were putting out a fire."

He shrugged, "Maybe."

"What did you see?"

"Something strange."

"In the smoke?"

"It fell from the sky and exploded on impact into a cloud, a purple cloud. That's when I saw her."

"Who?"

"It's too crazy. I can't tell you. Maybe I'm hallucinating. Hell, I don't even know if you're real."

He ran his fingers through his black hair and looked at the horizon behind him.

"Where are we? What kind of Hell hole are we in?"

Silence.

She observed him. He was young, probably under thirty-five, with a stocky, sturdy build and a strong, solid body. He had hazel eyes, abundant eyebrows, and a face etched with lines far beyond his years. She knew he had seen a lot.

"Firemen are heroes," she said. "I remember that much."

He listened.

"And since it looks like you and I are the only ones here, I have to call you something."

"You want to call me something? Is it a four-letter word?"

She laughed. "It is."

"Good. I feel like a four-letter word."

"You look like a 'Hero.' Okay, if I call you that?"

"Hero?" He mulled it over. "Heeeerrrrro. Hero. I like that. Herooooo."

"Okay, Hero. What do we do now?"

"Wait. You should have a name too. How about..."

"What? What are thinking?"

"Hmmmm," he searched the sky for a clue.

She noted the laugh lines around his mouth. He had a good sense of humor. What was he like when he wasn't fighting fires? Was he the life of the party? A good-time Charley? A big flirt?

"Mary? Susan? Nah. Blue? Nah. You're definitely not Blue."

"Nice try. You get a gold star for the last one. Very innovative. "

"Thank you. You remember lots of stuff."

"Just junk."

He paused a moment. "You know something. You're very pretty."

"I am?"

"Yeah. You got pretty eyes.

"I do? "

"Maybe I will just call you Pretty. Pretty One."

"Pretty One. Nice."

"Pretty One," he repeated. "I like it."

She smiled. She liked it too.

TOGETHER THEY WALKED in a direction that didn't have any particular appeal. All directions looked the same. Hero picked what he thought was South. He said it meant warmth and he liked the heat. She let him have the pick of directions because it really didn't matter to her which way they went. There was no way of knowing which horizon held what clues.

As they walked, she noticed her feet were not bothered by the rough texture of the cement, nor did she feel tired, hungry or thirsty. She was comfortable just as she was. There was little conversation between her and Hero. There was no need. Both were lost in their own thoughts. She knew they were wondering about the same things.

Images came to mind. Sunflowers and shimmering glass. Green grass framing a black pavement. Cardboard boxes. Traffic lights. Cold, steel train doors.

"An eye for an eye makes the whole world blind," Hero blurted out and broke her trance.

"What was that?"

"That's what she said, 'An eye for an eye makes the whole world blind.'"

"Who said that?"

"The woman with the scarves. After she told me that, she blew up."

"She blew up? As in exploded?"

"Well, not exactly exploded. She just turned into a ball of fire. Listen to me. That sounds crazy. Am I crazy?"

"I don't know. Are you?"

Maybe he was a madman, she thought to herself. But her heart told her something different. She knew he was telling the truth, his truth, anyway.

"What did she look like? This ball of fire?"

"Well, she looked kind of like a genie. You know, like a genie in a bottle with fancy scarves. Purple ones. And pink sequence with sparkly crap. She had these big eyelashes.

"She fell from the sky but didn't look like a woman at first. She was a blur, just a purple, and red blur. Disgusting. I thought, bomb. Then, there she was. A bombshell."

"Clever."

"She belly-danced her way to me and looked at me..."

Pretty One rolled her eyes. "Oh, please. She belly-danced her way to you? You sure you weren't dreaming?"

"Really. I swear. That's what I saw. You don't believe me?"

She sighed, "go on."

"Well, then she spoke in a really sexy voice and said that thing. That thing I told you."

"Then what?"

"Then she exploded into flames, and I had to put her out. I mean it out. That's when the rubble I thought I came out from disappeared. Then, you showed up. Weird, huh?"

"Weird, yes."

"Do you believe me, or do you think I'm nuts?"

"I have to believe you."

"Why? I'm having a hard time with it myself. Why would you believe me?"

"I have no other choice. If we have only each other, who else can I trust besides myself? I'll have to believe you if I want to trust you."

"You're smart. You're not only pretty, but you're smart too."

"Thanks. It's just logic."

"So, tell me what you think. What do you think it means?"

Pretty One gave it some thought. The sun's golden late afternoon light painted the concrete. They were heading into the night. At least that made sense.

"An eye for an eye makes the whole world blind means that getting even can only make matters worse."

"I'm not getting even with anybody. I'm just looking to get the hell home."

"Maybe the message is not for you. It's for you to tell somebody else." Pretty One said.

He stopped and looked directly into her eyes. "You amaze me."

"Why?"

"Because you're so wise. You look too young to be so wise. Who are you?"

"I told you, I don't know."

"How young do I look?"

"I don't know, twenty-something?"

They continued walking. Two lost souls without an identity, stranded in some strange place. She glanced at him, his eyes lost in some far-away path. What was this man like? Was he married? Single? Did someone somewhere miss him dearly?

And, who was she? Where did she live? Did someone somewhere miss her? Did she have a family? A child? A dog? How did she grow up? What did she do for fun? What was her favorite food?

She was a mystery to herself. A stranger. Was this a rare opportunity to get to know herself as if she were another person? To experience things objectively, without association or baggage? A being without a history, a name or attachments? Creating new experiences and seeing a world with fresh eyes? Reborn as a free entity. Maybe this was really her lucky day. Or not.

She walked beside her new friend as day melted into night, grateful for the company. The shuffling of their feet tapped an impression in the silence—a duet into the unknown.

CHAPTER 2

THE MOON'S LIGHT WAS bright. But it didn't reveal anything new. Pretty One insisted on camping out for the night. But Hero wanted to keep walking until they found something, anything that could change the status of where they were. Pretty One argued that it was too dangerous. She convinced Hero. They sat down on the cool concrete. There was no soft place to rest their heads, but they made do.

With night came the stars. But these stars were unlike anything Pretty One's semblance of memory recognized. The stars were like paper cut-outs with five defined points. It was as if they dangled from a giant mobile, on display with fiery neon colors. They were gemstones, rubies, sapphires, and emeralds against the velvet indigo sky. Close enough to touch. The full moon was enormous, like a circus balloon. It flooded the darkness with light, which cast Pretty One and Hero's shadows dark and defined against the concrete. In the glaring white light, Hero looked like a ghost. Maybe he was. Maybe they both were.

Hero reclined on the hard cement. The moon's eerie glow threw his shadow across Pretty One's face. The temperature was still comfortable, despite the lack of sunshine.

"Wishes," said Hero, "I used to make wishes on stars."

"You remember that?"

"But I don't remember stars looking like these. Like the ones up there. They're weird. They look stupid."

She laughed. Stupid stars sounded funny.

"They're a cartoon. I bet they have goofy voices, " he said.

"They look fake."

"Yeah, impostor stars. I want my real stars back."

"What if you remembered wrong? Maybe that's the way stars are supposed to look."

"Do you think so? Do you really think stars are supposed to look like those up there?"

"Don't you think it's funny, we can't remember who we are, but we remember enough to know that those stars are not right?" she said.

"So funny, I can't stop laughing." He wasn't laughing at all. "It's crazy. The whole damn thing. The rubble, the genie, the concrete. Even you."

"Me?"

"Not you. But you coming out of nowhere. I feel like an alien. I'm lost in space. Maybe I just lost it. I wish I knew what the hell was going on."

"Maybe that's it."

"What's it?"

"The stars. Maybe that's the wish we make. We'll make a wish on the stars, just like you remembered."

"You're getting girly on me."

"No, really. A wish...I wish...I wish I may, I wish I might have the wish I wish tonight," she said, surprised at the string of words that spilled out.

He sat up. "Star light, star bright. The first star I see tonight, I wish I may, I wish I might have the wish I wish tonight. I remember that," he said, excited.

Pretty One laughed at the gruff, brawny fireman reciting a nursery rhyme. "Who's girly now?"

He smirked, "Don't be a wise guy."

"What will you wish for?"

"Wish for? You're not serious."

"Come on, Hero. Have a little fun. What's your wish?"

"You go first," he said.

"Okay. I wish for," Pretty One offered, "I wish for answers, all the answers. Soon."

"Me too," said Hero, looking at a star.

"There. It's in the works," she said, talking to Hero as if he were a boy.

Hero looked at her with smiling eyes. They sent a message, not from a boy but from a man who was attracted to her. The look was familiar. She knew that look, though she couldn't remember from where or when.

"You look beautiful in this moonlight," he said in the softest voice he had.

He was interested in her, she thought. Was she being presumptuous? Was it only her imagination or was it her secret desire to be loved in a lonely place? She felt his eyes on her heart and looked away, feeling awkward. She had to trust her instincts, she told herself. It was the only thing left. Without a name or an identity, intuition was all she had. It told her that anything other than friendship would be dangerous.

"I like you. I really like you," he whispered.

She didn't know what to say. She didn't know him. He didn't know himself. She didn't know who she was and together, they didn't know anything.

Pretty One said nothing. She avoided looking at his eyes. But Hero looked at Pretty One anyway. He sighed.

"I'm sorry," he said. "You're just such a beautiful woman, and I haven't forgotten that I'm a man. That's all."

She nodded, flattered.

"We don't know who we are. We don't know who's out there waiting for us to come home. Maybe someone is missing you or me tonight," she told him. "We don't know. We don't know anything about each other or ourselves."

"You're right. Forgive me for being a guy."

"Forgiven," she smiled.

He resumed looking at the stars. "I remember wishing for something once. It's coming back to me, a wish I made." His eyes searched the sky as if words were hidden in the night. "I wished that someday, I would do something important. I was little. I remember sitting on a concrete porch in my backyard. It was really warm. I wasn't wearing a shirt. Clothes were hanging on a line. They weren't moving. It was that hot. And the stars, there were too many to count. They didn't look like those stars up there. They were tiny dots. I picked one and made my wish. I remember that."

"Wow, that's pretty detailed. Can you remember anything else?"

"That's it. That's all I remember."

"Do you remember if anyone else was with you?"

"Nope."

"I guess you can't ask for too much," she said. "Maybe it's coming back to you in bits and pieces. Maybe your wish is starting to come true."

"Can you remember anything?" he asked.

"Me? Well, I don't know. I remember odd, senseless things. Useless bits of information," she said.

"Like what?"

"Silly songs. Pretzel shapes. Warm breezes. An orange bathing suit. Yellow banana peels. Blades of grass. Train doors. Glass doorknobs. Meaningless sayings and... blue. I like the color blue. Like that blue star up there." Her eyes fixed on a particular sapphire stud. "I can't take my eyes off of it. I think blue is my favorite color."

"And you're so modest. See, you remember tons of things," he said and looked at the stars again. "I still have the same wish. I still hope I'll do something important one day. Whoever I am," he said and laughed.

"What are you laughing at?"

"It's just, I don't know. Making a wish on a star? Heck, I could be anybody. What if I was the president? Or what if I was a...serial killer?"

She wasn't fazed. "You're a fireman, remember?"

"How do you know?"

"Because of the clothes you're wearing."

"Why, just because I'm wearing a fire retardant suit, that makes me a fireman?"

"What else would it make you?"

"Does what I wear make me who I am? Is that what I've been reduced to? My clothes? I could be in costume, you know."

"It's a clue. At least you have a clue. Look at me. My clothes don't say anything."

"You're wearing black. Maybe you're an undertaker."

"An undertaker? Undertakers don't wear black."

"How do you know?"

"I just know. Don't ask me how or why. It's just another junk memory."

"Well, you look...you look professional. I guess that's the word."

"A professional what?"

"I don't know. Maybe you're an artist. Maybe a poet? Hey, what if we know each other. Did you ever think about that?"

"Anything is possible, I guess." she said, "I hardly think so, but who knows? Maybe you've read one of my poems."

"Nah, not me." he said, "Don't like that flowery crap."

"How do you know?"

"I just know. Maybe if you were a chef or something, I might have sampled your food."

"Food? I forgot about food."

"I know I like food. I'm not exactly a waif." He slapped his gut.

She laughed. She liked him. She liked his sense of humor. He was genuine. Whatever was on his mind came out of his mouth. He had nothing to hide. She liked that. It was okay to trust him, despite what happened before, despite his visions of belly-dancing purple genies. At least he was honest.

"Not hungry, huh?" she asked.

"Nope."

"Me neither."

"Though a nice cold beer would be good just about now."

"Beer?"

"Beer." he said, with a little thought, "Cold, frothy, pale and foamy, the ultimate thirst quencher."

"Are you thirsty, then?"

"No, not really. But do people drink beer because they're thirsty?"

"I don't know," she said, "You're the beer expert. Not me. I must not be a beer drinker."

"How about food? Do you remember your favorite meal?

"My favorite meal? How can I remember that?" she retorted. She couldn't even remember her name, let alone a meal.

"You remembered your favorite color," he said.

"Yeah, but that was just a guess."

"And you remembered the words to make a wish upon a star. You remembered that."

He was right, she thought. She remembered the Happy Birthday song too. Something popped into her head.

"Chocolate," she said.

"Chocolate?" His eyes lit up. "Tell me about your chocolate."

"My chocolate?" she thought, then understood what he meant. He wanted to hear her experience of chocolate, just the way he defined his beer. "Chocolate," she mused.

"Rich and strong and sweet, that's what I remember about chocolate. Sweet, romantic, dark, dense, sensual and there, it's so there. There was no questioning chocolate. It demands your attention and is courageous enough to be what it is. Chocolate has a presence. When it enters the room, you know it's there. It's loud and alive. That's chocolate. Creamy and powerful and versatile, no matter where it shows up. You either like it or not. There's no in-between with chocolate. It knows what it is and doesn't care what you think. That's Chocolate. It never pretends to be anything else."

"Wow," he said, mesmerized by her description, "maybe you are a poet."

She smiled, proud that she was able to summon up such a detailed memory. "Chocolate. I love chocolate. Do you?"

"Hmmm. I think I'm more interested in strawberry," he yawned. He relaxed on the cement, settling into the night.

"Are you tired?" she asked, wondering why she wasn't.

"Just a little."

She lay down next to him and sighed. She heard his breathing deepen. It was the only sound in the barren land.

"Hero?" she whispered.

He answered with a snore.

She stared at the sky, still wondering about the day's events. Just one day, this one day, changed everything. She was someone else just yesterday. She touched her stomach. Had her body given birth to life? She couldn't tell. What would that feel like anyway? Would her body feel any different if she was a mother? What was her culture? What was her religion? Did she believe in something profound? She looked down at herself again, her body illuminated by the moon's light. What

clues did her clothing offer? What was the color of her skin?
It was not too pale and not too dark. What race was she? It
seemed ambiguous. Where was she off to when she was struck
by sudden amnesia? Where were all the people? Where did
they go? Did the world end leaving her and Hero the only
survivors? An endless chain of thoughts. She was alive. She was
somebody. She knew that much. But exactly who?

At that moment, a star fell from the sky, twirling like a
corkscrew of paper cut from glittery material. The ruby red
shape danced toward her like an autumn leaf and landed on her
black shirt. She looked at it, wondering whether to touch it,
but the shimmering shape was too tempting. She picked it up.
The star was actually a leaf with a stem and five sharp points.
She looked at it in the moon's light and felt it. It was soft, velvet.
It smelled like fall.

"Hero?" She whispered, "Hey, Hero..."

He was in a deep sleep.

Maybe this experience was just for her.

SHE FLOATED AND COULDN'T breathe or see. It took
strength to open her eyes. And still, she couldn't see. Where
was she now? She panicked. Her heart pounded. What now?
She coughed. There was heat and smoke around her. The
choking fumes smelled toxic. She couldn't feel her feet. They
weren't on the ground. They were in the air. Was someone
carrying her? She felt the fabric of a rough jacket under her
fingers. She was aware of someone's strong arms holding her,
carrying her, the scent of his sweaty body mingling with the
smell of fire. There was a rumble. She felt the earth shake. Was

it an earthquake? Was there a fire? She couldn't breathe. She couldn't see. Where was she now? Where was her Hero? Help, a voice inside her head screamed, "Help!" she screamed aloud with the last morsel of energy she had.

THE WORD LINGERED ON her lips when Pretty One woke up. Her eyes snapped open and she gasped for a full breath of air. Breathe, she reminded herself. Breathe.

A Little Boy now stood over her.

She blinked a few times, disoriented. She fell asleep and had a terrible dream. Was she still dreaming?

No, the Little Boy was there. He was real. He stared at her with his big brown eyes. The boy was about seven-years-old.

"Who are you?" she asked and blinked a few more times to be sure he was really there.

"Help me find them," he said.

"Find who?"

"The rest of them," he answered, assuming she knew what he was talking about.

She sat up and looked for Hero. He was gone.

"Hero!" she shouted, "Hero!"

"He'll be back," said the Little Boy, confident.

"Where did he go?"

"Away," said the boy in his small, steady voice.

"Who are you?"

"Possibility," answered the Little Boy.

"Possibility?" she was confused.

The Little Boy's innocent face radiated goodness. His big, dreamy eyes were locked on hers. She realized this is no ordinary child and decided she wasn't afraid of him. She found his presence strangely peaceful. He appeared harmless, though something odd about him was different. He possessed a mystical quality. It was something beyond the edges of her reality.

"Where's Hero?"

The boy stared at her and blinked slowly.

"Where's Hero? Where's the man who was just here? The man who was sleeping right here, right here next to me? Did you see him?"

"Can you help me find them?" the boy asked again, in his soft voice.

"Who? Who are you looking for?"

"The rest of them. I can't find them. Please help me."

"Who? I don't know who you're looking for."

"Them. The ones who need to find me. I cannot find them."

The riddles were frustrating.

"How did you get here?"

"I was always here," he said. "That is why they need to find me. You, too, will need me one day," he said with the eyes of an old sage. "Once you are ready for me."

"What are you talking about? Please, Little Boy. I don't understand what you're telling me. Please, tell me the truth. I really don't want to play games."

"You will see," he said and walked outside the rim of moonlight, disappearing into darkness.

"Hero," she called again. "Hero!"

But there was nothing. She looked at the place where Hero had been resting. There was no trace of him or proof that he had ever been there. She sighed.

"Little Boy! Little Boy!" Her voice shook the silence.

Moonlight outlined the Little Boy's face. He stood small in the moon's light. But his shadow stood large.

"Little Boy," she asked. "Where am I?"

"You are on the Road."

"The Road? To where?"

"To the place you're supposed to be."

She paused.

"Where is that?"

"The place that's all around you and inside you." he whispered. "Whenever you are ready."

The Little Boy had a strange power over her. Maybe he had more answers. Maybe he knew all the answers. Or maybe he was going to drive her crazy.

"Do you know who I am? Do you know my name?"

"Yes," he said with a grin that revealed baby teeth. "You are Pretty One," he said.

How did he know that? Did he overhear her and Hero talking? Was he secretly watching them? But how? There was no place for him to hide, nothing but concrete and a naked horizon. How did he know? How?

"I have to go now. I have to find them all. We have to get ready," he said with seriousness beyond his age.

"Get ready? Ready for what?"

"The party," he giggled.

It made her smile. He was just a kid

"Can I come with you?" she asked

"If you are ready to play," he laughed and ran.

Pretty One chased him into the night.

PRETTY ONE FOLLOWED the boy out of the darkness and toward the dawn, which brightened the sky with purple and peach streaks. There, on the horizon, she saw a Tree. As they got closer, the details became clear. This Tree had hundreds of intertwining branches, as expressive as fingers. Some were thick and strong. Others were fine and wiry. Leaves sprouted from the top of the Tree's sturdy body. Its solid bark reminded her of Hero.

Where was he, anyway? Why did he leave her? Was she wrong about him? She hoped not because that meant that she could no longer trust herself. Her intuition was all she had.

The beautiful, majestic Tree had leaves that looked like the star that fell from the sky earlier that night. It seemed so long ago now. How long had she been asleep? Was the night here longer than the day?

There were different color leaves, just like the stars - blue, red, green, gold, purple, pink, yellow and orange. What kind of Tree would make a rainbow of perfectly star-shaped leaves? Pretty One noticed the Tree's roots were able to sprout through the concrete without cracking it, as if the cement were of dirt.

"Ask her," the Little Boy said.

"Ask who?"

There was no one there, just the two of them.

"Ask the Tree. The Tree knows."

"The Tree? You want me to talk to the Tree?"

"She knows everything. Ask her."

"What can I say to a Tree?"

"Listen then," said the Little Boy. "Put your hand on the Tree and listen."

Pretty One sighed. She had nothing to lose by asking the Tree a question. Nothing made sense here. Why should this? She placed her hand on the Tree's bark and closed her eyes.

"Listen with your heart, not your ears," he whispered.

She tried to listen, but her heart thought only of Hero. She missed him, even though he wasn't gone very long. They were so different, yet the same. She marveled at how she connected she felt to a man whose name she didn't know. Where was he now? Did he actually exist? Or was he merely a figment of her imagination?

Heck, she didn't even know her own name. She woke up in a land where no one had a name. What was a name, after all? Did it matter what his name was, what her name was, what anyone's name was?

Then she remembered a quote: "a rose by any other name was still a rose." She didn't know where it came from or whose words they were. Yet it was there, on the brink of memory, like the birthday song. Just another random tidbit of something from a past she didn't know.

If she knew her name, would it make a difference now? She was still who she was, no matter what her name. Perhaps she'd remember it one day, but it didn't matter just now. She was alive, regardless of who or where she was. But if she was who she was at this moment, a nameless being, was she any different than any other being? Didn't all spirits feel the same thing? Minus a name, friends, a history, what was the difference between her and any other passing, nameless soul? What was the difference between anyone? Wasn't everyone the same underneath the cloak of names and skin after all? Didn't every being feel love and loss, fear and hope, anger and joy? Was she no different than Hero? Could they actually be the same being?

Each thought was a spark of electricity. A strike of inspiration. Was she on to something here? Here. Where was here, she thought. Did place matter?

She was always here, no matter where here was. She was here in this moment, a time that was independent and unconnected to any other moment in history. There was no real proof of anything other than here, this minute, this now. Memory was a testimony of time, a survivor of the past. But without memory, was there any real evidence that then really did occur before now? Without landmarks and written history, was there indication that something actually happened before this instant? Without recollection, without photographs, without people, books and icons, was there really any proof of anything other than the ever-present moment? These things were the measures of time, the containers of experience.

Maybe nothing was real beyond this. Now was all she had. Without memories or clues, without even a friend to validate the past, did she really know if any thoughts or experiences before now were true? She was born here in the now. Maybe there is nothing before and nothing after, no yesterday or tomorrow, just a perpetual present. It all made sense now. Nothing mattered but this experience. This now.

But still, she couldn't help but dive into the then, plunging headfirst into a vast unknown, with only her imagination as a guide. Could she conjure up a past? Could anyone do that?

Does everyone's perception of the past have to be the same? Did she really have a past? Words came to her mind, as they had before. A voice told her she was the "Spring after the Winter."

When she opened her eyes she realized she said those last words aloud. While she thought she was thinking, she was really listening. She listened with her heart to the Tree. Or, maybe she just listened to her heart. She wasn't sure.

She removed her hand from the bark and said, "Thank you."

The stoic Tree said nothing, even though Pretty One expected a reply. She looked for the Little Boy, but he was gone. Just like Hero. She was alone again. But this time, she wasn't afraid because she understood now that no matter how challenging her experiences might be, she still had herself. She plucked a purple star leaf from the Tree's branch and tucked it into her back pocket. Someday she would show someone, just to prove this moment had existed. It was her signpost in the road of time, a trophy to mark this encounter, just to prove to herself if no one else, she was really here.

The sky was brighter. She was determined to find Hero, she headed toward the bright horizon.

CHAPTER 3

PRETTY ONE CHOSE TO walk South, at least the direction Hero thought was South. Occasionally she looked back to remind herself the Tree still existed, watching it grow smaller until it disappeared. This must be the earth, she thought, since the surface seemed to be round enough to engulf objects on the horizon. A silly thought, but she questioned everything here. This idea gave her comfort and hope. Something else just might pop up on the horizon the way the Tree did.

She walked for miles, she guessed. There was nothing in front of her, and now, nothing behind her but endless pavement.

She still wasn't hungry, even though she couldn't remember the last time she had eaten. She wasn't tired, sweaty or disheveled from the walk. The sun warmed her shoulders. The breeze was delicious and fragrant, even though there wasn't a flower in sight.

Her thoughts wandered back to the Tree with the vivid leaves and silent wisdom. She checked her pocket for the purple leaf. Still there. It was her receipt of the experience, a confirmation that then existed. That she existed then. She tucked the leaf back into her pocket.

Where were the answers. Where was Hero, the Little Boy, and where was she going now? What was her fate?

Just be, she said to herself. Something guided her from within. Just be, it said. The answers will come.

She took a deep breath and stopped. She looked at the horizons around her, then started toward the east. Something told her to change course. She didn't know why, but she trusted and followed.

A breeze combed through her short hair and ruffled it enough for a strand to fall in front of her eyes. She took note. Her hair was dark, almost black. She held it in front of her face as sunlight shimmered through the shiny strand. Her dark hair was another clue. The breeze grew stronger. In it, she thought she heard a voice. Pretty One stood still and listened as the wind pushed at her back. There was a sound in the wind, a whisper, a word. Something. She listened.

"Pretty One," it seemed to say."Pretty One," it called louder. She knew the voice and gasped.

"Hero!" she shouted"Hero! Keep talking!"

The wind carried his voice to her ears as she rushed toward the eastern horizon.

PRETTY ONE CAME UPON something in the distance. Hero's voice led her to this point. She listened for him to call out for her again but heard nothing.

An exotic palace glistened on the horizon. Two ornate towers. An unfamiliar architecture. There was nothing else around it, no grass, no garden, no trees, no statues and no people.

Pretty One paused. Then moved toward marble stairs, which led to an open-arched doorway. It was dark inside.

Should she go in? She closed her eyes. Took a deep breath. And, stepped inside.

It was enormous, majestic and dimly lit by dancing candles along the walls. Rows of wooden, gothic pews faced an altar. Incense overpowered her senses triggering a glint of memory. She had been here before. But couldn't remember where or when.

High ceilings amplified her breath as she walked bare footed on the cold marble floor. It was old, musty. The artwork reflected different cultures and beliefs. Giant stone pillars with gold-leaf trimmings supported a domed ceiling painted with a blue sky and clouds. The tall, sapphire glass windows bore colorful stars, like the ones she had seen with Hero the night before.

"Hello?"

Her voice echoed. She heard her voice. "Hello?"

"Hello?" A man's voice answered.

Pretty One startled. She wasn't alone. A man wearing a brown robe sat in the front, reading.

"Hello?" she whispered.

He read aloud. "How lonely sits the city that was once full of people. How like a window she has become, she that was great among the nations. She that was a princess among cities has become an empty vessel."

The man turned to her and offered a big, kind smile.

"The Lamentations, 1.1," he said and shut the book. "Hello there."

Pretty One walked closer to the older, bald man with cherry cheeks. His presence was inviting.

"Take a seat here," he indicated with a friendly tap on the wooden pew. "Have a seat next to me."

She sat beside him. A tattered book lay open on his lap.

"You're looking for someone, aren't you?"

"How did you know?"

"Everyone is looking for somebody," he said.

"Who are you?"

"Father Mike."

"Father Mike," she repeated.

"Yes, Pretty One?"

"How did you know my name?"

"Is that your name?"

"Well. Not really."

"Then, tell me your name."

"I don't know. I mean, I don't remember my name."

"That's okay. You don't need a name to exist. Many things have no name yet they exist."

"Like what?"

"Like this place. It doesn't have a name. But it exists. Think of all the things that have never been discovered. Does that mean these things don't exist?"

"I don't know, Father. I never thought of it that way."

"Something can still be, even though it doesn't have a name. If you can't see something, does it exist?"

She thought about his question. Maybe he was helping her find the answers. If you can't see something, does it exist?

Well, she couldn't really see her face, but she knew it existed because she could see and breathe and move her lips to speak. She couldn't see her voice, but she knew it was there. She heard her echo just moments ago. She couldn't see time but somehow knew it was real."

"Yes," she answered, "I guess you're right."

Father Mike smiled. "Now that's faith."

She was proud of herself. She liked this new stranger. There were so many strangers here, more survivors of whatever happened. At first, she thought there was only Hero and herself. That they were the sole survivors of an unknown catastrophe that annihilated the world they knew and left them without memories or a home.

"What happened, Father Mike? What happened to everyone? All the people left? Where are they all?"

"Oh, there are lots of people here. You just haven't seen them, that's all. Maybe you need new eyes?"

"New eyes? What for?"

"So you can see. They're all here. They're all around you. They're right here now, but you can't see them."

Pretty One looked around.

"Oh, you'll see them. Eventually." Father Mike laughed. "They'll find you if you don't find them. All in good time, my dear."

"Where are they now?" she asked.

"They're looking for their place, I suppose. Aren't you?"

"I'm looking for Hero."

"Hero? I've never heard of him. Is he supposed to save you?"

That is an interesting way of putting it, she thought. "No, Hero is my friend. He's a fireman."

"Oh, a fireman. I saw a lot of firemen come through here, at once, a while ago. Maybe he's with them."

"Where did they go, do you know?"

"Most likely on the Road."

"Father, I'm confused. Where is everyone going?"

"Ah, child. You too are on the Road."

"The Road to where?"

"Now that's a question. Some say it leads to a person. Some think it's a place. But to me, it leads to a state of mind."

"I don't understand, Father. This is all very confusing. Where are we anyway? What is this place called?"

"Don't worry, my dear. It will all make sense soon enough."

"And why all the concrete? There's cement everywhere. Why?"

"It's solid and sturdy. A durable surface for a Road well traveled."

"Well traveled? I haven't seen many people at all."

Father Mike smiled."It will all make sense, I promise you."

"But these people. Where are they all coming from?"

"Then. They're coming from then, the place before this," he said.

He somehow accessed her thoughts. She felt vulnerable.

"You needn't be afraid now," he said. "You're past that. Fear is the enemy. Once you're rid of the fear, hope is all you will see. Remember that."

He brushed a tuft of white hair from his forehead. He had a beautiful face. Warm, amber eyes. Thick, black eyelashes. Perfect teeth. Laugh lines around his mouth and eyes. This man held joy and peace. He was magnetic. Joyful. Familiar. Like a favorite uncle. She noticed a thick, gold ring on the third finger of his left hand. Was he married? Or devoted to his faith?

"You see, you're on the Road already," he said.

"On the Road?"

"Yes."

"That's what the Little Boy told me last night."

Everyone is looking for the Road. But you're lucky. You're on it already."

She sighed.

"Heaven is within yourself. That's the key."

"The key? To what?"

"Hope. Souls can't thrive without it. You'll find yours. And you'll find your Hero too. But he's not on the Road."

"He isn't? Where is he, then?"

"All the answers will come. Be patient, Pretty One."

"Does that mean bad things for him?"

"No. Not all all."

Silence.

"Does that mean bad things for me?"

"No, no, no," he chuckled.

"Phew. Thank you, Father."

"Go, Pretty One, Find your place. Remember. You're beyond fear now. You will be fine, no matter what."

He gave her a thumbs up.

"Goodbye, Pretty One. And, good luck." Father Mike tucked the book under his arm, got up and left. She watched the hem of his brown robe sweep the marble tiles as he climbed the two steps to the altar and swiftly exited through a red velvet door without turning back.

She was alone again. She stared at the red door. Where did that lead? She was hesitant. Father Mike left her with more questions than answers. She got up, took a breath, and approached the altar. Stone statues stood guard. She looked up at the towering figures. None of them had eyes. Except one. The one with a boyish face. The statue looked familiar, even though she hadn't seen it before.

She caught a glimpse of herself in a window's reflection. And froze. There she was. A young woman. Dark hair. Dark eyes. Nice teeth. A small nose. She looked like a nice person. But a stranger. She stared at herself, burning the image in her mind.

There was a sound. It startled her. She looked up.

"Hero!"

"Pretty one!" He shouted.

CHAPTER 4

"WHAT HAPPENED TO YOU?"she hugged him

"I don't know. A hell of a ride is all I can say. A nightmare."

"What happened?"

"I'm just happy to see you again."

"How did you find me here?"

"I heard you calling me. I followed your voice here, to this place, whatever this joint is," he said. "How did you get here?"

"You're not going to believe it, but I followed your voice here too."

"You heard my voice coming from this place? How can that be when you were here first?"

"Do you really expect me to explain that? I'm just happy to see you, that's all."

"Likewise. Now, can somebody tell me where the hell we are?"

"We're in the place with no name."

"Of course," he laughed, "so what else is new?"

"Hey, look at this," she said. There was something on the floor by her feet. She picked it up and studied the the old, brass skeleton key that hadn't been there before.

"Look at this. 104. What do you think that means?"

"Let me see," he said, took the key and studied the number that was etched into the surface. He had to look at everything simply because he believed nothing. Pretty One knew that about him and wondered if he had always been that way. But then, she thought, she needed her own kind of proof too, like the leaf in her pocket.

"Well, look at that. Maybe it's the key to here. This place, this whatchyamacallit place."

He walked to the giant, old oak door at the entrance and tried the key. The opening was a diamond shape, nothing remotely similar to the key's head, or to any normal lock he had ever seen.

"Nope," he said, "doesn't fit here. It's just another random piece of junk. Might as well leave it where you found it."

"I think we should keep it. You just never know when we'll need it." She tucked it in her pocket, another souvenir of the moment. She wanted to tell him of her experience at the Tree, of her theory, but knew he wouldn't understand."

"IF you want to carry around a piece of junk, that's up to you."

Hero looked around. "This must be a church or something like that."

"I don't know. But, there was someone." Pretty One stopped. Should she tell him?

"You saw someone?"

"Yes," she said, following her intuition. Yes, it was all right to share this information.

"A priest. A monk. Some kind of religious guy. He was here when I first came in, sitting on the pew over there."

"Must be a Church."

"He asked me to call him Father Mike."

"Not Brother Mike or Friar Mike?"

"Don't be a wise guy."

"Where is he? Where did he go?"

"He left a few minutes before you got here. He had a premonition you were coming."

"Yeah? What else did he say?"

She paused and observed him. He didn't look well.

"Are you okay?" She sat next to him.

"Yeah, yeah. I think I have a fever."

She felt his head but he was cool. But then again, nothing made sense here.

"Father Mike said I was on a Road."

"To where?"

"To...I don't know. A person. A place. A state of mind?"

"We're on a Road? What Road?"

"No," she said. "He said I was on the Road. But you weren't."

"What do you mean? I'm not on the Road?"

"That's just what he said."

"Well, to hell with that. Who needs to be on some stupid Road? Maybe it's the Road to hell."

"Hero? What are you saying?"

He sighed. "I'm sorry. I'm losing my mind. I feel nauseous. I didn't mean you were going to hell. I'm just done with this. All of this. I can't take it anymore."

"What happened in your dream?"

"Nightmare."

"What happened?"

"I woke up in a hospital room. It was dark. Quiet. No one was around. There was only a nightstand with a statue of Saint Jude on it and a candle. A small blue candle."

"How did you know you were in a hospital?"

"It looked like a hospital. Smelled like a hospital. It was so real. Maybe it was real. I had a paper bracelet. But I couldn't read it. I tried, but I couldn't. I knew it was my name. I knew it. If only I could've read that damn thing, I would have known everything."

"Not everything," she said. "Who knows what was on that bracelet. A name is just a name. What does it matter if you are Joe or Harry if you don't remember what's associated with that name? You're still you, no matter what your name is. You're always you."

Hero listened. Tired, he rested his eyes.

"There was something else," he said. "Something written on the base of the statue. It said, 'Give us hope.'"

"Hope. That's what Father Mike said."

"Hope. What's that supposed to mean to me?"

"When you think all is lost, that's when you need hope the most. Especially when nothing makes sense."

"And that's supposed to make sense?"

"Father Mike said, once we rid ourselves of fear, hope is all we'll see."

"Are you saying I'm scared? I'm a fireman. I don't get scared."

"Cut the macho stuff. You can't tell me you're not just a little scared. Come on, Hero. Be honest with yourself. Father Mike said we just have to trust everything will work out okay. And once you trust that invisible force inside you, you'll feel nothing but hope. Hope that things will work the way you've imagined. Fear is the enemy of hope. That's what he means. You can't have one when you have the other.

"What else did he say?"

"So much. He was so wise. I really liked him. He made sense. He said we were beyond fear now. Heaven is within."

"Within us, huh?"

"Trust your insides. Your gut," she said.

"And what about this Road you're on?"

"I don't know."

"This is all just bizarre."

"Maybe we're dreaming."

"Dreaming? You think this is all a dream?"

"Maybe."

"Look, I'm pinching myself, and I'm not waking up. This is no dream, my friend."

"Hero, stop it."

"Where is Father Mike? I want to talk to him."

"You don't believe me?"

"I don't believe anything I can't get my hands around."

"Put your hands around me."

"Yeah?"

They paused.

He grabbed her and held her tight.

She hugged him back.

They held each other in silence.

Hero silently wept.

She held him tighter.

"I can't take it anymore," he whispered.

He broke away, wiped away a tear. "I'm sorry."

"No, it's alright," she whispered. "Maybe we can find him. Father Mike."

"Where is he?"

"He left through that red door."

She didn't notice the details of the door before. It was a padded sparkling red vinyl door with rivets and an ornate wrought-iron handle.

"Look at this door. Will you look at this? It's a joke." Hero pulled it open. It popped open.

"It's just a closet," he said. "This is just a closet. Look."

"A closet?" Pretty One looked at the small closet that contained a robe on a hanger and a pair of old, worn leather shoes on the floor. "This is what Father Mike was wearing."

"Well then, a naked, holy guy must be hiding somewhere here."

She laughed. Then wondered. Did Father Mike really exist? She had no proof other than his words. "I saw him leave through this door. Where did he go?"

Pretty One walked away from the altar and sat in the front pew. Hero followed and sat next to her. "Purple Genies and Monks. Sounds like a bad movie."

"You're feeling better, aren't you?"

"Yep. Sorry about that. A few minutes ago."

"It's okay. You're human."

They sat in silence for a little while. Pretty One checked her back pocket and made sure the leaf was still there. It was, along with the key. Yes. She decided to believe Father Mike existed. The key, the Tree, the Little Boy were as real to her as Hero was. As she was.

"Who's to say what's real?" Hero proposed.

"Are we a philosopher now?"

"No. A poet."

"Poet Hero. Nice to have you back."

He smiled. "I was just thinking about how I had my Genie. You had your Friar. Or was it a Monk?"

She laughed.

"Oh, by the way, I saw my Genie again. Last night."

"Don't tell me. She was dancing for you at your hospital bed."

"No. Much worse. But first, let's get out of here."

OUTSIDE, A CITY SKYLINE stood in the distance.

"Now, where did that come from?" Hero said.

Pretty One walked toward it with confidence. Hero followed.

The city was farther than it looked. As they walked, Hero shared the details of his dream:

He woke up in the middle of the night and saw a fire not far from where they slept. He didn't want to wake Pretty One, so he went, alone, to investigate the flame. The closer he got to it, the farther the flame became. He didn't realize it was leading him astray until it was too late. By that time, he was so far away he couldn't find his way back to Pretty One.

When he looked again, the fire right there in front of him. Before he had a chance to run, it exploded into the Purple Genie. The Genie approached him looking at him with purple eyes that stared at him through layers of scarves. He asked her who she was. "You are not here," she whispered before she vanished in a puff of smoke.

The next he knew, he woke up in a dark room. The bed was comfortable, and his pillows were soft. He felt disoriented. He saw a flickering candle on the nightstand and the statue. He was so tired. He must have dozed off.

The cold concrete under his face woke him up. He heard Pretty One calling him. That's how he found her.

"Maybe it's a memory. Pieces of your history are coming back," she told him. It was the only thing that made sense.

"But why did she tell me I wasn't here? Where would I be if I am not here?"

"Maybe you don't want to be here."

"That's true. I don't want to be here. Do you?"

"I don't have a choice. Do you?"

Hero shrugged his shoulders.

Pretty One and Hero were not in the city. They followed a main street through a canyon of tall buildings. It was a city made of structures from different eras: old brownstones with fire escapes, shiny steel high-rises with modern designs. Two white towers presided over the rest; monuments that sparkled in the afternoon light.

"Wow," Pretty One said. "It's an oasis."

"Or a mirage," added Hero. "Nobody's here."

He was right. A city this large should be bustling with people. Where was everyone?

As they walked through a narrow street between buildings they noticed all the windows were missing glass.

"I have a bad feeling," he said. "Something terrible happened here."

"We're okay," she whispered.

The closer they got to the white towers, the more dust they saw. Thick, gray dust collected in the curbs and between the cobblestones on the street. Dust covered abandoned cars on the narrow streets. It stuck to their feet. The dust became so thick it turned into fog. It smelled terrible. They waded through ankle-high stacks of white, torn paper, mixed in with the dust. It looked like snow. It collected on windowsills, fire escapes and everywhere. A message written into the dust on a car read: God help us.

What happened in this city? Was there a war? A bomb? Some kind of attack that eradicated people but left buildings standing? It was like the moment when she first awoke. She was covered with dust, too. What did it mean and how was she connected to this place? There had to be a link, but what?

Hero quietly observed, trying to solve the mystery. He was a fireman. He had instincts she didn't have. She waited for him to share his conclusions. She thought about what Father Mike said. She didn't have to be afraid of anything anymore. There was nothing left to fear, she thought. The message was strong. She felt no fear, no anxiety, just calm. Whatever happened to this city didn't scare her.

Traffic lights flashed green, yellow and red. A dusty street sign bore the word "Liberty" in fat, white, bold letters. She still remembered how to read. And knew what the words meant, even though she didn't know who she was. But what was the language? Liberty was the state of being free. She had liberty. She was free from past pain, guilt, and mistakes. She was free from the burden of identity. She was free from hunger and thirst, free from responsibility and debt. She was free, she thought. Were the people who once lived here free? Was Hero feeling free?

"Liberty" was the only signpost they saw. The other streets were unmarked. Pretty One wondered how people found their way around without signposts and street names. How did they give others directions? Without signs and symbols, didn't people get lost?

She didn't have any sign posts here, though. Did that mean she was lost? She didn't have a name or a map. But she did get messages; an inner voice that led her through the way, keeping her from getting lost. There were signs and symbols all around her if she kept her eyes open. She received directions from the power inside her. If she used her inner guidance as a tool, she could decipher the language of this foreign world. Even though the clues and signals had meanings that she didn't fully comprehend. She had to find the system, she thought, the rules and functioning of this world in order to understand it. Cracking the code was the key to understanding anything.

"This street leads directly to those two buildings," said Hero.

They were almost upon the entrance, where Liberty Street ended. A paper on the ground caught the afternoon sun. She picked it up. Its burnt edges looked like a design. A hand-written message read: Help! We can't get out!

"What's wrong?" Hero saw her staring at the paper. She showed it to him.

"Strange, he said, then became alert. "Fire. I smell fire. There was a fire."

"What do you think happened?"

"I'm a fireman, not a psychic!"

There was a sound. Low and rumbling, like distant thunder. It shook the ground. They froze.

An airplane cut through the blue sky. The sound was loud. Even though the plane was just a speck in the sky.

"Signs of life," she squinted, following its path in the sky.

"Not really. Nothing makes sense here. Why should that?" Hero grew more irritated.

"You're right," she said.

"Damn it. How do I let go of what makes sense?" he asked. "How can I make decisions? How do I do that? Tell me, smart girl, how do I do that?"

"I don't have the answer."

"Go ahead, call me crazy. But it bugs me once in a while, that's all."

"I know," she said. "Where to now, Captain?"

He sighed and continued. She followed him toward the towers. Pretty One admired the magnificent pillars, amazed at the work that went into creating it. There were windows at the top of each, barely visible in the sky. She wondered how something could touch the sky and still be on the Earth at the same time. She wanted to climb to the top so she could be in heaven while still on earth.

Then, white dove flew out from a window. Pretty One took it as a good omen as she watched the bird become a spec of white in the blue yonder. She didn't bother to share the experience with her friend.

Hero walked around and found an entrance. He pushed the dusty glass door but it was jammed. He pulled and it opened.

"Huh," said Hero, "says 'push.'"

He held the door open. "After you."

Pretty One entered. There was an odd smell. Everything was covered in dust. In the lobby was a broken phone and one office chair.

They wandered through large pillars and decorative archways. She noted the dead plants wilted in giant glass buckets. Their footsteps echoed in the cavernous lobby and their footprints revealed a marble floor beneath the dust. Modern light fixtures overhead lit the way.

"Look, electricity. Someone must be here."

Hero approached an elevator with caution. Pretty One watched him. There was only one button, the arrow pointing up. Hero pressed it and waited. The whir of elevator gears kicked in. Red lights above the brass doors displayed floor numbers, from 104 to 1.

"104," whispered Pretty One. She remembered the key. "The 104th floor."

Giant doors flew open. Hero and Pretty One hesitated. Where was it going to take them? The doors remained open, waiting. They looked at each other. Without a word, they stepped inside the elevator car.

The doors shut quickly. The elevator moved on its own, taking them somewhere of its own choosing. None of the buttons they pressed worked. They couldn't do anything but watch, wait and hold on.

The numbers in the window flickered so quickly, it was a blur until it stopped at 104.

"The key," Pretty One said, "the same number as the one on the key."

Hero said nothing. The doors opened. They stepped out into a dark vestibule. A shag rug covered the floor. The walls were pale and empty. A hallway led them toward glass doors.

"Where are we?" Pretty One said. "What do people do here?" A dim fluorescent light flickered overhead. There were no logos or signs.

"Shall we?" Hero suggested and pulled open the door.

Just as they were about to enter, the phone rang. They froze.

It rang and rang on an abandoned desk, begging to be answered.

"Don't do it," said Hero.

Pretty One picked it up anyway. "Hello?"

"I'm not going to make it," said a man's quivering voice. "Just tell her that I love her."

The line went dead. Pretty One hung up.

"What happened? Who was it?"

"I think people are dying here,"she said in a somber voice.

"Maybe they're already dead."

"A call from a ghost? That's a strange thing for you to say."

"Thought I'd break the mold. Not be so predictable."

She smiled. Maybe the impressions of the dead still lingered in this building, she thought. Maybe that's what happened to places where people died. Their spirits become embedded in the walls, in the air, in a desperate attempt to prove they were once here. Who was the man who reached out from the grave? When was he here? Hero picked up the receiver.

"What are you doing?"

"I'll see who called." He paused.

"What?"

"Geez Louise, nothing makes sense. These buttons don't make any sense. No numbers, just random letters." He slammed the receiver down.

The phone rang again.

"We're not answering it!" Hero pulled her into a hallway. It was a windowless maze. She kept thinking about the caller, his desperate attempt not to be forgotten, to prove that he truly existed somewhere in time.

The maze ended at a door labeled 104.

"104," Pretty One said aloud. She took the key from her pocket. The key's number matched.

Hero tried the handle. It was locked.

Pretty One tried the key. The door opened. They looked at each other.

Hero walked in first, slow and cautious. Pretty One followed.

It was a bedroom. Exotic. Sheer curtains billowed from glassless windows. Ornate rugs covered the marble floor. A king sized canopy bed in the distance. A Young Man with a long beard rested was hunched over in anguish, his face hidden in his hands. The Young Man looked up.

"I am sorry," he whispered.

Pretty One wondered if he was real. He wore a white, gauzy robe. He was handsome and gentle.

"Forgive me," he whispered. "Please forgive me."

"For what?" asked Hero.

"I didn't mean to do it. I didn't know what I was doing," he sobbed.

Pretty One and Hero looked at each other, baffled.

"I know life is valuable, no matter whose life it is. I knew that. I'm sorry." The Young Man looked directly at Pretty One. She felt a chill. Was he a ghost?

"I stole your destiny. I am so sorry."

"My destiny?" She felt ill.

"What's the matter?" Hero asked her.

She shook her head. "Nothing."

"What are you talking about?" Hero asked the Young man.

"Ask her. She knows what I mean."

Pretty One looked out the window and saw only sky. It was like they were in heaven, yet somehow still tethered to earth.

"Beware of those who do onto others as they would not have done onto themselves." The Young Man said. "Remember this message. It is the measure of all things true. Remember what I say. Tell the others."

"Tell who?" Hero asked.

"Them, those of the earth. Tell them we are all the same inside. It makes no sense to hate others. It means we hate only ourselves."

"Who are you? What is your name?" Hero fired.

"My name doesn't matter. My message is what counts. I warn of fear. Fear causes hate. Hatred is ignorance. Ignorance robs souls of destiny, and steals the light from the world. Tell them that."

Hero turned to Pretty One. "Do you know what he's talking about?"

She did. She understood. It was same thing Father Mike said. Fear is the opposite of hope.

"I must go now," he said. "Remember what I told you. Remember to tell them all," he said to Hero.

"Why are you telling me?" asked Hero.

"Because you have time to tell them."

"I don't understand."

"Ask her." He pointed to Pretty One then left the room and shut the door.

They stared at the door for a moment. Sheer curtains billowed in the window. It was silent.

"What do you know that I don't know?" Hero asked Pretty One.

"An eye for an eye makes the whole world blind," she said. "I don't know why I said that."

Pretty One traced the Young Man's steps to the door and opened it. It was an empty room with stone walls.

There was a large painting, a portrait of the Young Man, gaunt and pale, surrounded by seven homely, older women with unhappy faces.

Hero laughed. "Nice girls." He looked around and spotted another door. He pulled it open. A sea of concrete. Everywhere.

"Well, now this looks familiar." Hero joked.

"Well, not exactly," she said. This concrete was different. It had metal doors in the ground. The sky was gray.

"Where are we? On a roof?" Hero said. He ventured out. Pretty One did too. Cautious. Suspicious. Uncertain.

A door slammed. They looked back. The door they came from was shut. There was no doorknob, no way to open it again.

They were locked out of one world, trapped in another.

They looked around. A chilling sight.

A cellar door flipped open and slammed shut.

"Did you see that?"She asked.

"I did."

A series of cellar doors flapped open and shut, as if choreographed. Hero and Pretty One grabbed onto each other. The clammer sounded like thunder. Then, silence.

A cold breeze ruffled their hair.

Then, one door squeaked open. All the way. After a beat, something emerged.

Hero and Pretty One watched in suspense.

A zombie-like creature climbed out, dressed in eighteenth century garb. Another door opened. A gaunt, lifeless woman wearing a bonnet emerged. Behind her, a child came out from another door, holding a dirty doll.

"This was not real!" Pretty One shouted. There was no proof of this moment. She didn't want any. She tried to forget it. Hero's hands crushed her arm.

She opened her eyes. A dozen zombies stared at them.

"There's nothing to fear," she said aloud.

Hero stared, frozen.

"Hero?" She nudged him, "Snap out of it!" She shook him. But he was lost in a lifeless stare. She shook him until he snapped out of it.

"Are you all right?" she asked. "Are you okay?"

"Yes. I think."

They were surrounded by morbid bodies. Where would they go from here? There was no way out. Then, she saw it.

"Look," she pointed.

"What?"

"An open door. Our only escape."

"Escape to where?"

"Out of here."

They dodged the zombies and headed straight for an open door in the ground.

"Can't wait to see what's behind door number three," Hero shouted.

They jumped into the unknown. The door slammed closed behind them.

CHAPTER 5

THEY CLIMBED DOWN INTO total darkness. Pretty One reminded herself not to be afraid .

"You okay?" Hero whispered.

"Yep. You?"

"Fine."

As they descended, a shaft of sunlight fell spilled over them. The air was salty and sweet. They heard the sound of crashing waves.

Pretty One stepped into warm sand. It felt good. She looked up, and realized they were under a boardwalk. She stepped back. It was a beautiful day. Clear blue skies and fluffy clouds.

"Yes, a beach!" Hero shouted and ran to the shore. And froze. Pretty One caught up with him. Hero stared at the crashing waves.

"I remember. Swimming on a windy day. Choppy waters. I swam against the current, toward someone." He paused. "But I didn't save her."

"You saved her," Pretty One whispered.

"I didn't. I saw her head bobbing in and out of the water. Then, she was gone."

"You saved someone," Pretty One said. "You saved me."

He smiled at her.

"You saved me too."

They held hands and watched the sun glistened on waves. Wind tussled their hair.

There was something familiar about this moment, she thought. She sat with someone on a beach somewhere in time. But with who? Whose hand did she hold once before?

They sat on the soft, warm sand to rest. It felt real, as she sifted granules through her fingers. She tasted the salt on her lips and crunched on sand fragments. She tucked a pinch of sand into her pocket. Proof. For some future reference.

"Those people up there. They were dead." Hero said.

"Why were you in a trance?"

"They were trying to make me one of them. They wanted company, those bastards. Thanks for rescuing me."

"No problem."

"Did you feel it too?"

"Um. No."

"Maybe it was my cologne."

She laughed. "They needed cologne, that's for sure ."

"I like the beach," he said, soaking in the sun.

Something fell out of the sky and landed in the water with a giant splash.

"Wow, did you see that?" Hero asked.

"It looked like a shoe."

"A shoe?"

It happened again. A black pump landed inches away from Pretty One.

A blue sneaker fell next to it.

"What the hell is happening? It's raining shoes." Hero looked up.

A red shoe fell. She tried it on.

"Look, it fits."

"Shoes are falling from the sky, and you're thinking about shoe size? "

"If the shoes fit. Right?"

"This is crazy. Maybe this isn't such a good place."

"Look, another red shoe." Pretty One tried it on her other foot. "Too big."

"Shoes are not supposed to fall from the sky."

"Dead people aren't supposed to rise out of cellar doors."

Suddenly, a shower of shoes. Hundreds rained down, splashing into the water and pounding the sand. Shoes of all kinds. Dirty, dusty, worn shoes. Men's, women's, children's, shoes of every style, shape, size and color. The shoes pelted them.

Pretty One tossed off the shoes. They ran for shelter under the boardwalk. She saw a sign in the distance: BAR.

"Look," she shouted, pointing at the sign.

"A bar?"

"Come on!" She shouted. They headed toward the sign over a wooden door.

"What's with the doors in this place?"

There wasn't a handle on this door. Pretty One pushed it. They entered.

It was not a bar but the ruins of an old subway station. It was dark except for the wedge of light that snuck through the cracks. It smelled of ammonia. Two words remained intact in mosaic subway tile ruins: WORLD and ENTER.

"Bar? Where the hell is the bar? I can use a drink. Especially after getting caught in a shoe storm!"

"Maybe bar is short for another word. Or maybe it's only a remnant of a word."

"What word? A bar is a bar. And a bar isn't an archeological dig."

"Maybe it was short for barricade, or barrow, or barter, or barber, or barbaric."

"Or barf. Because that's what that smell will make me do if we don't get out of here soon." He looked to the right. "Let's follow this, see where it goes."

Pretty One stared down the dark tunnel. "Why?"

"Why? You want to stay here and inhale this stink? I've had about enough stenches for the day. Come on."

Hero pulled her into the path of abandoned rails. They disappeared into the darkness. They could barely see each other, but the held on, listening to the sound of pebbles beneath their feet.

"How can you see anything?"

"Feel that," he said. "Under your feet. A train track."

She felt it. Cold. Steel.

"Let's follow it," he said.

"But what if a train comes?"

"Oh, we'll know if a train is coming."

"But where would we hide?"

"Who cares, let's go."

It was getting brighter.

"Well, look at that. There is a light at the end of the tunnel."

She found that amusing. "You see the light?"

The tunnel lead them to a turnstile. They pushed through it and entered a room, an ornate station, with marble pillars and gold leaf trimmings. A gothic brass ticket booth stood in the center. A giant clock displayed time in roman numerals. 8:50. A big blackboard listed. ARRIVALS and DEPARTURES.

"A train station," she said.

"No kidding," he said.

"Where is everyone?"

Hero called out. "Hello?"

"Hello," someone answered.

It startled them.

"Who's there?"

"I'm right here," a man in a red tuxedo and a carnival hat waved from the Gothic booth. "Come one, come all!" he shouted."It's just around the corner. Make sure you meet your party now."

"Now where did that dude come from?" Hero whispered to himself.

"What's around the corner?" She asked the man.

"The party. I always say, if you're invited to a party, go. Keeps you alive."

"Our party is meeting us at the party?" She said. "That sounds like fun."

"Who?" Hero shouted. "Who's 'our party'?"

"You'll see," the man said.. "Just follow the exit signs, and you'll see it." The man grinned like a clown. Pretty One giggled.

"What's so funny?"

"That guy," she couldn't control her laughter.

"Laughter is the salve of the soul. Laugh all you want. Laugh even more at me. Laugh, laugh, laugh!"said the man.

"Bizarre"

The man pointed at the exit sign. "There."

SHE WAS SURROUNDED by strangers who all recognized her. Even though Pretty One had no idea who they were. How did she get here? Where was Hero? Again they were separated. But how? She searched for him through a crowd of smiling faces.

"Hero?" she shouted. "Hero?"

The people surrounded her, reached for her hair, her clothes, and her hands. She pushed them away. "Who are you?"

"It's us, honey. Don't you remember?" An older woman wearing red lipstick said. "I'm aunt Mary."

"Who?"

"And I'm uncle Ralph," said an older man.

"I don't know who any of you are," she turned away from them, still in search of Hero.

"You can't go back to him. He's no good for you," aunt Mary said.

"Hero!" She shouted.

"He's not your friend, missy. Just someone who's holding you back," said uncle Ralph.

"Holding me back from what?"

"You'll never get anywhere if you stay friends with him," said the aunt.

"You will kill him!" said a sturdy middle aged woman.

"Kill him? What?"

"That's what you're doing to him unless you stop it right now," she said.

"Listen to her," said the uncle. "She's your grandmother."

"Grandma? Seriously?"

"Grannie, actually."

"If you're my grannie, then what's my name?"

"Pretty One, of course."

"My name is not Pretty One. See, you don't know me."

"How do you know your name is not Pretty One? Grannie grabbed her arm.

"No, my name is not Pretty One. Now let me go!" She broke away from the woman's grip.

"You don't remember me?" Grannie said, disappointed. "Let her go. She's not ready yet," she told the group.

For a split second, Pretty One recognized the woman's blue eyes.

"Be careful out there," Grannie told her. "I hope you come home soon."

The crowd vanished, disappearing one by one.

And then there was Hero standing in front of her as if he had always been there.

"What just happened?" she asked.

"Nothing. We just walked in here, and you froze. Are you okay?"

"You didn't see the people?"

"What people?"

"The older people. So many of them."

"No," he said. "No one else here but me and you and that carnival freak."

She saw the empty room.

Hero pointed to the sign: BAR.

"There it is. Come on, I think we both could use a drink."

59

A PARTY. A BAND. A spinning disco ball. Musicians rocked the place. People from all walks of life danced to music.

"Wow, so this is where all the people are," said Hero.

"It's so loud in here. I can't believe we didn't hear this music in the other room."

"What?"

"Never mind."

They brushed by people, but it was as if they were invisible. Pretty One deliberately stared into a man's eyes. He clearly didn't see her. What was going on now? She grabbed Hero's hand and shouted into his ear. "They can't see us."

Hero tapped a woman on the shoulder. She didn't react. Hero pushed a burly man. The man didn't flinch. Hero dropped his pants, revealing his undies. No one noticed except Pretty One. It gave her a good chuckle.

"REFRESH YOUR SOUL!" A Bartender shouted into a microphone from a podium behind the bar. He bore a strange resemblance to Carnival Man. "Refresh your soul. Come here and quench your thirst for life."

"May I help you?" the Bartender asked Pretty One and Hero. He had no trouble seeing them.

"What's today's special?" Hero asked.

"This evening's specials are Fresh Eyes. We're sold out of New Eyes. We have Fresh Start and New Day on tap. We also have a Cold Truth and a Sobering Tonic if you're interested. What'll it be for you and the lady?

"I'll take what's on tap."

"May I suggest a Cold Truth for you, my sir," said the Bartender. "And Fresh Eyes for the lady with beautiful eyes?"

The Bartender produced two colorful, bubbly drinks in crystal glasses. "Two excellent choices. Here you go."

Pretty One took the sparkling beverage, which looked more like a science experiment.

"Drink up, my friends, before these delicious drinks go bad," The Bartender insisted. "Savor every sip because no two are alike."

"Don't drink it," Pretty One whispered to Hero. She had a bad feeling. Something wasn't right.

"Nothing to be afraid of. Go on, drink up, my friends. The most delicious flavors in the universe are right in your glasses. Creamy, smooth and refreshing. Try it."

Hero clinked his glass with Pretty One.

"Oh, what the heck," Hero said. "Bottom's up!" He winked at her and threw back the drink in one gulp.

"Hey. Tastes pretty damn good," he said, licking his lips.

"See, I told you," said the Bartender.

"Try yours."

Pretty One shrugged. Nothing here mattered anyway. There was nothing to fear. She wanted a drink. So, she drank the Fresh Eyes. It was cold and refreshing, even though she wasn't thirsty. She remembered Hero's comment, You don't have to be thirsty to enjoy a tasty, refreshing drink.

They ordered another round.

CHAPTER 6

PRETTY ONE WOKE UP in bed, in an unfamiliar room. It was night. Crickets chirped. She sat up. Where was she now? How did she get here?

"Hero?" she called out. No answer. Gone. Again. Her head hurt. She felt sick. She should have never had that drink. She should've followed her intuition.

She breathed in the aroma of a fireplace. It was comforting. She was in someone's home. But whose? Who stoked the fire? She noticed a photo on a dresser nearby, with a small candle and a flower vase.

She picked it up. It was a framed poster with "MISSING" in large, simple letters above a face in silhouette. Why would anyone frame a terrible shot where you couldn't see the person's face? Beneath the photo, a handwritten note: WE LOVE YOU. COME HOME.

"Hello?" She called. "Hello?"

Nothing.

Moonlight cast its rays on the dark walls from a nearby window. She looked outside. A large backyard. Leaves on the ground. A small flower garden. Was it autumn?

She heard a sound and swiveled around.

"Hello?"

Was it an animal? A person?

Pretty One stepped into the hallway. The carpet was soft under her feet. It smelled of fresh paint. The hallway lead to a closed door. The sound was coming from there. Was someone crying?

She pressed her ear against the door, then gently pushed the door. It opened. She saw a man in front of a crackling fireplace, his face buried in his hands. She didn't want to intrude. This must be his home.

She tiptoed toward him, but he didn't notice. There were cardboard boxes stacked in a corner. Empty walls. Did he just move in? Or was he moving out?

"Hello?" she whispered.

He didn't respond.

"Hello?"

He didn't see her. She noted his silver wedding band.

Was he like the people at the party, unable to see beyond their own Reality? She was getting used to being invisible.

He seemed familiar, but she wasn't sure why. She felt like she knew every crease of his face, the veins in his hands, every curl in his hair. She knew this man. But who was he?

She touched his hair. She was attracted to him. He tapped his head, suddenly aware and looked around but didn't see her.

"Sweetie?" he whispered. "Is that you?"

Was he talking to her?

"Can you see me?" she asked.

She noticed his unshaven, rough face, his dark tired eyes glistening in the fire's light. Had he lost someone?

Pretty One put her arms around him.

Just be, she remembered. Let the moment unfold.

He wiped his eye and looked around. "If you're here, say something. Move something. Give me a sign."

What should she do? She could kick something and give him a sign. A sign that someone was here. Even though it was the wrong someone. But why give this poor man false hope? He was already in pain. She was tempted. Perhaps it would make him feel better. Some hope is better than no hope at all. She remembered Father Mike's words, "Spirits cannot exist without love, purpose, and hope." So she knocked over a glass. The man jumped, petrified.

Pretty One ran out into the hallway, wondering why she did it. The poor guy thinks the person he was talking to actually responded. She felt bad and thought about Hero again. Where was he? She noticed a light under a door. She pushed it open.

"Come in," said a woman sitting a desk, dressed in dark clothes, with her back to Pretty One. She was writing.

"Are you ready?" the woman asked, without turning around.

"Ready? Ready for what?" Pretty One asked.

The woman swiveled around.

"Are you ready to move on?"

Pretty One saw the young woman with dark hair and dark eyes, wearing the same clothes she was wearing.

"Who are you?" asked Pretty One.

"You know who I am," the woman said.

Pretty One paused.

"You really do, but you're afraid to admit it.

"Are you...me?"

"Every you is me. Every me is you. We are all connected. We are each other."

Pretty One thought about the Young Man who said the same thing.

"What is your name?" Pretty One asked.

"Wisdom."

"Wisdom?"

"Wisdom," said the woman. "That's my name. I am the one who speaks to you."

"It's you?"

"I have all the answers."

"Then, please, tell me who I am."

"You are the light of the world," answered the woman. "Listen. I speak without words. That is me. That is me, being you. I am the part of you that lives forever. Listen to me and I will help you."

They caught each other's eyes. Pretty One was listening. She listened to the Tree, and she listened to her heart.

"Please tell me."

"Trust what you hear. You will find your answers when you are ready."

"Who am I?"

"You know who you are. Everyone's been telling you, but you are not listening. You have to listen beyond what you can hear."

"Where is my Hero?"

"Listen and follow," she said. "But don't listen for something that is not there. Let the voice find you."

She listened. She heard nothing. Another riddle. Why so many riddles?

"The man inside. Who is he?"

"You will know when you are ready."

"Why can't he see me?"

"Because he can't see you doesn't mean you don't exist."

"You're confusing me."

"Listen and you will hear."

Silence.

Pretty One closed her eyes and listened. She listened with her heart as the Tree had taught her to do.

"Pretty One," Hero's voice called her name. It was what had saved her before. She was sure it would save her again.

"Hero." She said and opened her eyes.

Wisdom was gone.

Pretty One went to the desk. One the paper was a word: BELIEVE.

"Believe?" she whispered to herself. What was she supposed to believe? What could she believe? Nothing made sense.

"Pretty One!" Hero's voice called.

"Hero!"

"Help!" Hero shouted.

She followed his voice to an open door that lead to a basement.

CHAPTER 7

"HERO!" I'M COMING!" She followed his voice down the stairs. She heard muffled voices, then an alarm. She tried not to fall in the dark and held on to the hot walls.

"Hero! Hang on!"

The ground shook. She lost her balance and tumbled downstairs. The light went out. Now, it was completely dark. She felt for the stairs and stood up on a flat surface. She was okay. The lights blasted on. She was now standing in a lobby.

A television poised on a counter displayed a horrifying image: raging flames bursting from two giant, white towers. It sent plumes of thick black smoke into the blue sky. People plunged from windows and exploded on the ground. Chaos. Screams. Sirens.

The television went out.

The lights went out.

"Hero!" she yelled into the darkness.

PRETTY ONE OPENED HER eyes. She was again back where it all began, on the cement surface under a clear, blue sky. Hero lay a few yards away, sprawled out on the ground as if he had fallen from the sky. He was covered in so much dust he looked like a ghost.

"Hero?"

She got up and started toward him. As she did, she noticed she was wearing a silver ring. It wasn't there before. She touched it. Then looked to Hero.

"Hero?"

He was breathing. Maybe he was sleeping. Or unconscious. Or maybe she was dreaming. She kneeled beside him and wiped the white dust from his face. He let out a snore. She sighed. He was just asleep.

She slipped the ring off her finger and saw an inscription inside: September 17, 2000, To Lucy with love. Forever, Frank.

Lucy and Frank? Who were they? Why was she wearing their ring? She slipped it back on her finger. The answer would come, she guessed.

Hero stirred.

"Dad?" he mumbled.

"Hero," she whispered. "Wake up."

His eyes flew open. He stared at her.

"Hero? What's the matter?"

"Who are you?

"Who am I? What do you mean who am I? Don't you recognize me?"

"Where am I?"

"Come on, Hero, stop kidding around."

"Who are you?"

"Pretty One, remember? You called me 'Pretty One.' What's the matter?"

He rubbed his eyes. His head fell into his hands.

"Where's my father?"

"Your father?"

Hero sprung to his feet and brushed off the dust.

"I remember now," he said. I couldn't breathe. I couldn't see. I was looking for my father. I was looking for my brothers. I remember."

Hero seemed different now. Something changed.

"I don't understand what happened."

"Do you remember the bar?"

"I ordered a Cold Truth. Maybe that was it. I don't know."

"Maybe we were drugged."

"Maybe." He noticed the ring. "What's that?"

"I woke up with it."

"Yours?"

"I don't know. I feel like I've always had it." She saw something on the horizon.

"Look, do you see that?" Pretty One pointed.

"Maybe it's a mirage. Maybe I don't see a thing."

Pretty One smiled. That was the Hero she knew and loved.

She walked toward a crowd of people in colorful attire marching toward them. Each person there held a piece of paper with a picture of someone. On each picture was a giant word: "MISSING." There were all kinds of people congregated there. All looking for someone.

"I FOUND HER!" A JOVIAL woman shouted from the crowd, wearing a flowery flowing outfit. She greeted Pretty One with a warm smile and a big hug.

"What?" Pretty One squirmed away from the embrace.

The woman held a MISSING poster with a picture of Pretty One.

Hero looked on, "Hey, where's my hug?"

The woman grabbed Hero's shoulder so he didn't feel left out and smiled at both of them.

"You are not missing anymore, my dear," she told Pretty One.

"Who are you?"

"I am Speranza. Your guardian."

"My guardian?"

"Yes. Everyone has a guardian, visible or invisible. You had me worried for a minute there."

Finding Speranza was like finding a long-lost favorite aunt.

"I'm your escort. Come with me," she said and took Pretty One's hand.

"Where are we going?"

"Home!"

"Hey, what about me?"

Speranza tapped him affectionally, "Don't worry, there will be a place for you."

"Come," she told Pretty One, "I'm taking you home."

"Yes, finally!"

"Come, I will show you your Promised Land."

"My Promised Land? I thought we were going home."

"Oh, my dear," laughed Speranza. "Everyone has a Promised Land. That is your home."

"Hero, you hear that? I'm going home!"

"Nice. Can I come along for the ride?"

"Oh, I'm afraid this is not for both of you. Pretty One, this is your Road. Everyone has a Road. Hero must find his way back to where he came from."

"He doesn't know where he came from."

"Don't I have a Road too?" he asked.

"You do, Hero. You must follow your Road back," Speranza said.

"Well, where's my guardian to show me the way?"

"Wait. Let me see if there's someone here for you," Speranza searched the photographs people were holding. But there were none of Hero.

"I am sorry, young man. But there is no one here for you."

Hero looked around for himself, disappointed.

"He has to come with us. I can't leave him here alone after all we've been through together," Pretty One told Speranza.

"I'm sorry, my dear, but this is best for both of you. Trust me. For you too," she told Hero. "Someday, you'll thank me. And so will your family."

Pretty One remembered what the people at the train station said. Was it true? Could she kill him by dragging him along? Would he hold her back? Perhaps this is what they meant.

"Sometimes, the best thing to do is also the hardest. Once you are over the hard part, the going gets easy. This will be hard for both of you, but it will be the best thing you'll ever do for each other. Really, it's the best thing," said Speranza.

Pretty One knew she was right.

"It's your time to go, my dear Pretty One. It's your time, but it's not Hero's. Come. This is your moment. Right here, right now. Hero will find his way. As soon as we leave, he'll find it. But if you are together, each of you will be forever lost. You must go your separate ways to find your way."

Pretty One hugged Hero.

He wrapped his arms around her too, accepting his fate. "I will miss you. You, my Pretty One, have been my hero all along."

Pretty One couldn't let go. Would she ever see him again?

Hero broke the embrace. "Go. Don't worry about me. I'm a fireman. I always find my way out of danger."

Pretty One wiped away a tear. "Goodbye, Hero. My Hero."

She turned to Speranza. "I'm ready."

She looked at Hero one last time.

"I will be all right. I promise. Now, get out of here. Go home already."

Her eyes welled up. "Wait." She said and went back to Hero. She plucked the star-shaped leaf from her pocket and handed it to him. "Here. Proof. That I was real."

"I promise you will see your Hero again and it will be even better. But now, you must set him free. In the end, you will both be happy. You will see." Speranza said. "It's all good."

"Go home, and don't forget to send me a postcard!" He shouted.

Petty One smiled through her tears.

Speranza took Pretty One's hand and led her toward the horizon.

Pretty One looked back and watched Hero grow smaller on the horizon until he disappeared.

"I KNOW YOU ARE SAD right now, but you will find your answer soon," said Speranza.

Pretty One walked in silence, lost in thought.

"Sometimes, the Road to your Reality is an unexpected path," said Speranza. "You must be willing to take the hard choice to reach your destined nation."

"Can you tell me who I am?"

"You know who you are, my dear. You have all the answers. You always did. You are just not ready for them."

Pretty One sighed.

Speranza stopped.

"What?"

"Shhhh," said Speranza. "Listen."

They stood still.

"Can you hear that?"

Pretty One heard it. A rumble, like a distant train, but human too.

"What is that?"

"Don't be frightened. Listen. Just listen."

Now it sounded like a voice.

Pretty One listened but didn't understand.

Speranza pointed to the ground.

Bubbles rose from the concrete and floated to the sky.

"The sound is coming from here." Speranza put her ear to the concrete. Pretty One did the same. They heard it.

"I love you," said a muffled beneath the concrete, "I love you, Lucy."

Pretty One plucked her ear from the concrete and took the ring off to read its inscription again.

"Lucy. I'm Lucy!" Pretty One whispered.

CHAPTER 8

A HOUSE ON THE HORIZON. A small garden. A large lawn. An oasis in the concrete. The scent of fresh cut grass and lilacs. Birds. It was spring.

Speranza led Lucy to the door.

Number NINE marked the house address.

"It's open," said Speranza.

Lucy pushed the door. They entered.

She remembered the city and the poor Young Man with the ugly brides. She remembered Father Mike, the Little Boy and the Tree that said so much. It was all so far away now. Where were they? Where was everyone?

It was quiet inside. It smelled of fresh paint. Unopened boxes stacked in the corner. Minimal furniture. Lucy walked through the rooms. She knew this house. The house she had been in before.

Speranza followed Lucy down a hallway toward a bedroom with a neatly made queen-sized bed, a night table and a dresser. Lucy picked up the framed picture on the nightstand. A happy couple on their wedding day. Lucy wiped a tear, sat on the bed and put the picture back. Speranza sat next to her.

"Am I dead?"

Speranza smiled.

Was she dead? Dead? Dead! How could she be dead?

"No, my dear. You are very much alive."

Lucy sighed, relieved.

"You're alive in the hearts of those who love you and you will live on in them forever. Love is life and life is love."

Lucy broke down. She was dead. She cried for herself and for the things she would never experience. For the children she would never have. For her husband, who she missed so much. For her family. And for Hero, the strength behind her existence in this strange place.

But how could she be dead? How could she be dead when she was breathing and thinking and feeling?

"How can this be? How can I be dead? I don't understand."

Speranza lifted Lucy's face.

"Smile, my dear. You will soon see that this is the only life that matters. It is not your name or your house, or your belongings. It is your spirit. You never will die. You have only evolved, that's all."

"It is like when you are born. At first, you are scared and unable to understand what is going on, but then it becomes the only way you know. The same is true of when you die. You will get used to it. Then you will never want to go back again," Speranza took Lucy's hand. "You will wonder how you got anything done while lugging around a physical body. It needs so much care."

Lucy laughed. Speranza had an odd sense of humor.

"Come, Lucy," Speranza said.

"Lucy." The name was so strange to her now. She had gotten used to her name as Pretty One. But now, she knew her name was really Lucy. People called her Lucy all along and she only allowed herself to hear Pretty One. The Little Boy, the dead relatives, Father Mike, they all knew. Yet she wasn't listening.

"Lucy," she said aloud.

"Come, let's continue our journey. Let's join the others."

Lucy gazed at the wedding picture again. Speranza put her arm around her.

"Come, Lucy."

"Others? There are others?"

"Yes, many others," she said. "Come, they're waiting for us."

She was Lucy the Pretty One. She was Lucy, the ambitious young author driven to success. She was Lucy, the wife and Lucy the new homeowner. It was all coming back. She closed her eyes once more. A flood of memories. Speranza waited, allowing her to experience them.

"It was just starting for me," she said. "My new husband, my new home, the home of my dreams. I can't believe it. I just can't believe it. I was having lunch, and that's the last thing I knew. Lunch. Why did I have to have lunch that day? I never eat lunch."

"You can't blame yourself, Lucy. It was your time to go."

"Why? Why was it my time?"

"I don't know. Nobody knows that but you. Ask yourself. Your Wisdom will tell you only when you're ready to hear the answer."

Speranza got up. Lucy did too, with one last look at the photo. "Frank, how could I forget you? How could I leave you? My Frankie, I can't believe you were not on my mind for one second. I miss you and I love you."

Lucy left with Speranza.

CHAPTER 9

SHE REMEMBERED EVERYTHING. That last moment, the final conversation with her husband. What was for dinner? That was the last thing they talked about. Food. It all came back to her. In the middle of chaos and fire alarms, she remembered screaming "I love you" into her cell phone. She left message on a recording. What did Frank do once he got it? She didn't know. She remembered the staircase, fire and smoke. The trembling walls and floor. Trying to find the exit.

She remembered the final draft due to the publisher that morning. She was behind because of the move and worked through the night. Deadlines were her motivator and she worked best under pressure. She was tired on her last day and wondered if she had not been so tired, would she still be alive? Was the book worth her life? What was it about anyway? A dissection of destiny, a study of why and how, things unfold in a lifetime. What had made her spend years on this subject? It was ironic.

She remembered the novel she was reading on the train on her way to her lunch meeting. Everything was symbolic for her. The story was about two lovers living in different worlds, wondering if they would ever see each other again. She was only halfway done with it. Did they meet again? She would never know. There was just so much to remember. The dinner

Frank made when she finally sold her book. The chocolate soufflé fell flat in the oven.

What was she doing going downtown, of all days throughout the year? Why did she pick that day and place to have lunch with her agent? She picked it. She picked it. Did her inner Wisdom lead to her demise? Why would it do that to her when it was her only trusted friend, the single survivor of her life before this world.

Peter, her agent, didn't want to do it that day, but she had pushed for it anyway, eager to hear what news he had for her. That was how she was, impulsive, decisive and impatient. That was how she was. Who was she now?

Her thoughts drifted back to when she and Frank bought the new house, the home of their dreams. Good fortune fell out of the sky and landed on their laps effortlessly. That was an example she used in the final draft of her book. That was one way destiny worked. But why couldn't she explain away the thing that took her life? The walls of the house were bare and white. She told Frank they had to be mango, even though he insisted beige was really more appropriate. They painted every other wall in a mint color that just made the Mango pop. The color combination made her happy. Frank liked to see her happy.

She felt lucky and content. She had a loving husband, a wonderful home. She had been a writer all her life, from the moment she could speak her first words told a story. It took her so long to finally reach her aspirations because life sometimes got in the way. Distractions sometimes got the best of her. For the first time in her life, things really started to happen. They planned to get a dog, a chocolate Lab, sometime next year. She just bought a book about puppies and had a name picked out. Fudge. She thought about him, about them, she and Frank. They were barely married a year, with their anniversary only one week away. Her life, which seemed so charmed, had come to a screeching halt, squashed flat, for no apparent reason. She liked to believe everything worked out for the best. Did it?

Her mind wandered back to that dreadful day. Her last day. Those words were hard to believe. Her lifetime as Lucy Casie Smith was over.

She thought of Hero. Then, it hit her.

During her last moments, she remembered someone picking her up in the middle of all the chaos. She was barely coherent and in so much pain that she couldn't move. This person carried her through the smoke and down crumbling steps in a dark stairwell. Though she could not see her rescuer's face, the strong arms that held her tight felt familiar and safe. He was the fireman who had attempted to save her life. She now believed this man was Hero. Her Hero. She smiled at the revelation. Even before she was Pretty One, they were connected while she was still Lucy. But who was he really? Was he dead as well?

Then she remembered floating. She was as light as air and felt like a cloud, looking down through cotton eyes, peacefully hovering over a big city. She saw the confusion, smoke and fire. There were fire trucks and flashes of light. But from her point of view, everything moved in slow motion.

Through the white plumes of smoke, she caught a glimpse of transparent faces lingering in an ever-present cloud that remained over the place from which it was born. She didn't know who they were, but she wasn't frightened by the thousands of faces that emerged from the dark clouds surrounding the land below.

How long had she been up there? The clouds grew thicker, that much she remembered. They became murky and dense. The clouds completely obscured her vision until she couldn't see anything but white mist. That's when her memory went blank. She didn't know what had happened immediately after that or how much time went by. When she finally woke, she found herself on the concrete sidewalk. She had all her answers now, as Wisdom had promised. She had all her answers except for Hero. Who was he? Where was he now?

THEY WALKED FOR A LONG time. She was deep in thought. Speranza didn't interrupt Lucy's daydream. Instead, she provided calm companionship down a path unfamiliar to Lucy.

When Lucy awoke from her daydream and returned to the present, she discovered the ground was soft. Sand. A purple sunset spilled over small dunes. Speranza told her they were getting closer now because the concrete was softening and it was getting easier to walk. Lucy enjoyed the sensation of the warm, smooth sand against her toes. "Closer to where?"

"Your Promised Land. Your new Reality," said Speranza. "Your hope."

Hope was something she certainly needed. She was transfixed by the peach purple sunset and warm, easy sand. It was a kind of heightened reality. Everything was so super real. It surpassed anything her imagination could have dreamed up. It was intoxicating. She felt lightheaded and giddy. The warm breeze felt delicious. She sucked in the scent of roses in the air. The colors were vibrant. She couldn't remember anything like these colors. They were brighter. They were vivid. They were alive. This experience seemed more real than anything she had ever experienced.

"Where are we going again?"

"Home. It is where you will find the others."

She burst out laughing. "I'm sorry, I don't know why I'm laughing," she said. "I have nothing to laugh about."

Speranza started laughing too. "Why avoid a laugh when you don't have to? You have plenty to laugh about, Lucy."

They walked for a while longer as the sunset melted into the indigo night. Their giggles dissolved into tranquility with the soothing night. The moon was round and large, guiding them with its soft, powdery light.

Lucy remembered the night she gazed at the stars with Hero. She thought about him and their conversation as she observed the same stars, glistening like rubies and sapphires in the velvet sky.

This was her Reality now.

"Reality constantly changes and yours eventually will too," Speranza told her. "Someday you will forget your experience as Pretty One and as Lucy. Instead, you will just BE."

This made Lucy sad. She didn't want to forget Frank, Hero, or anyone else she loved. Who would she be if she wasn't Lucy or Pretty One?

Speranza assured her that it wouldn't matter. She wouldn't care. "Do you think a tree misses its autumn leaves when it's blooming in spring? Your destiny unfolds as you exist," Speranza told her" and you will move on to new revelations and identities. Yet, through it all, you will still be you. It will make sense. You will see."

"Was I here before too?"

"Never here, in this present time, no. But here in-between realities, yes. You just don't remember."

"Who was I before this?"

"You were so many things."

"So many things? What was I?"

"Oh Lucy, I can't tell you. You have forgotten them for a reason. You are here now, BE here and BE in this moment. Your inner Wisdom knows what it needs to learn without having to rehash it all in the now. That is why it knows how to guide you. It's taken the essence from all your experiences and only what is important for your growth. You don't need anything else. The rest is a distraction."

"What about Hero? Who is he?"

"You will find that answer too. You will know soon."

"Is he dead too?"

"You are both alive."

"Is he here?"

"He is not HERE, not in the same HERE as you are. "

"Can you tell me where he is now?"

"All in good time, Lucy, all in good time. Be patient."

Lucy looked at the sky, chose a glistening sapphire star and made a wish. She asked the star to help Hero find his way home. She made a wish for Frank, that he will find peace in his new life without her. She had to make one more wish since three was her lucky number. She wished for courage to accept this unexpected way of life, to find happiness here. As she made these wishes, she remembered her nickname, Lucky

Lucy. That's what they used to call her, even when she was little. Her aunts and uncles thought it was cute. But was she really lucky after all?

Memories rose to the surface, so many flashed through her mind. They demanded attention as if they knew it was their final chance to prove their existence before they became extinct forever. These were her memories as Lucy, as Pretty One. They were dying too. Or transforming, as Speranza liked to call it. She thought back to the older people who surrounded her at the train station and now remembered who they were. Those men and women were beloved relatives who had passed on during her life. She remembered them clearly now, though they seemed like obnoxious strangers when she met them. Aunt Mary died when she was just five. She remembered hearing the news of her aunt's death. It didn't make sense, even when her mother explained that Aunt Mary was going to heaven and could not come back. She couldn't understand why her aunt would go away without being able to make a telephone call. Death was an incomprehensible state to a five-year-old who believed she would live forever.

Then, there was Aunt Frannie, who had died last year, just before her wedding day. That made Lucy sad. Aunt Frannie was the kind of relative who insisted Lucy get married. She questioned why she wasn't married at every opportunity. It was a shame her aunt missed out on the big day. Her Grandmother. How could she have forgotten her? She was wise and loving, her mother's mother who made her own pasta and read tarot cards. She always told Lucy she would lead a charmed life. Was Grannie wrong? Had Grannie always known how short Lucy's life would be and secretly wept for her? Grannie passed when

Lucy was in her twenties. That death took a lot out of her, she remembered. She cried for five days straight and wondered if she would ever smile again. But life went on, as it always did, and Lucy lived her life, wrote her books, and found love - and death. Would she see Grannie again? Speranza thought so.

Lucy wondered about her parents. Where were they now? She was certain they felt deep, inconsolable grief. She was their only child and they lived for her. She was their everything. What would they do without her now? How could she tell them she was okay, that she was still alive? Why wasn't there a way to communicate between worlds that was as easy as picking up a phone? Why didn't that technology exist? She knew there had to be a way of communication, but no one had discovered it yet. There wasn't a name for this communication tool that she believed would someday be a way of life for everyone in all realities. That had to happen. There were just too many smart people in both realities. Someone would figure it out. Perhaps she would be the one.

She searched the sky and made a wish on another star, a gleaming white one. She knew this broke her "three-time" rule, but it didn't matter anymore. Nothing mattered because she was dead. She could do anything she pleased. She gazed at the white star then closed her eyes. What was the one thing she really wanted right this minute? She wanted a hug, a cuddle, a loving embrace that said everything would be okay. The kind of embrace she could hide inside. She knew where she could get exactly that. Frank. She made her wish. She missed curling up beside him, his loving little kisses that always made her feel better, no matter what kind of day she had. His love for her was Lucy's salve. It was her cure for everything. That was her

Frank. She opened her eyes and looked at the star again. How could she be dead? It was beyond her comprehension, beyond her realm of knowledge.

"Come on, Lucy, we have to keep moving," said Speranza.

"I'm sorry. I know I've been holding us back."

"No apologies, my dear. You need to take an assessment of your life. Everyone does when they're on the Road. The Road is the place to find lost memories and undiscovered realizations. Ponder all you want, my dear. This is the place to do it. But we must keep moving."

Speranza and Lucy continued to walk, their bare feet sinking into the warm sand. Lucy observed her companion. She was warm and filled with light, the combination of every relative Lucy had ever loved.

Speranza was short and heavy and wore a long flowing caftan with a purple print. Lucy couldn't tell if the silky, draped dress that older ladies wore when they tried to conceal their fat had a design of flowers or paisley. Speranza's face was wide and open, her eyes were dark and large. Her skin was dark which made her bright pink lipstick pop.

This was the first time Lucy had the chance to really notice her companion. She was so immersed in sorrow and confusion she really hadn't looked at Speranza the way she observed her now. Speranza was beautiful, with a full head of gray curly hair. The kind of person Lucy could entrust her life with—or her death.

"Speranza, were you ever on Earth?"

"I am on Earth right now."

"You mean you're alive, in the flesh?"

"Just because we are here does not mean we are not on Earth. We are still on Earth, my dear."

"How could we be in Heaven but still on Earth?"

"Heaven is a part of Earth. It is just one of the many dimensions of existing. There is so much for you to learn."

"Then, are you like me, Speranza? Were you made of flesh too at one point in your life?"

"No, Lucy. I was never made of flesh. But you and I are still the same. We are both living spirits."

Lucy had to really think about this. Speranza was so real, so human.

"I know how confusing this must be. I look like everyone else you have encountered in your life, and I am, with one exception. My Reality has always been here. I never needed to exist in the flesh, in the way you are thinking."

"Were you born here, then?"

"You can say that."

"Were you ever a little girl?"

"No, Lucy. I was always who I am now. I know that may not make sense to you, but I was always like this, what you see right now."

"Are you an angel, then?"

Speranza giggled, "Oh, I like that. I like when people call me an angel. But we are all angels, really. You too."

"What do you do here when you're not with me?"

"I live like you do. I live for my job and my family."

"You have children?"

"Oh, many of them."

"Where are your children? Do you have a husband too?"

"No husband, just plenty of children. Some who look older than me too." Speranza smiled, amused. "You're one of mine."

"Me?"

"I know, I know, it is all very unusual to you. But I am your guardian through your Realities. I have always been there for you."

"You have? How come I've never seen you before?"

"Have you ever seen anyone from any other Reality before? Did you ever see your Grannie again after she passed?"

It made sense to Lucy now. Lots of things were making sense now.

"When you are busy transitioning between Realities, I work with my other children."

This made Lucy think even more. It was nice to get acquainted with her guardian Speranza. It explained why she was so instantly comfortable with her. She was familiar. But, despite all this, Lucy still felt a growing sadness. She thought about the people she would never see, kiss, hold or love again. Would they go on with their lives and forget all about her? In years to come, would she a faded memory that no longer triggered an emotion? Would Frank move on and marry someone else? Would he have children with another woman and forget all about her? Lucy was worried that she'd disappear from the memories of those she loved and become an invisible entity without proof she existed? Did she really exist at all? Lucy couldn't hold back the tears.

"What is wrong, my dear?"

"I just don't understand. Why me? Why did this all have to happen? I just want to go home. I miss my home. I miss my life. It happened too soon. I am too young to die."

"Oh, dear, dear," Speranza said, wrapping her arms around Lucy. "Sometimes, there are no answers for the things that happen."

"But why? Why did this happen to me?"

"This is how your life unfolded. There is no one to blame. All the events happened just the way your spirit, your inner Wisdom, planned it."

"I did this to myself, then?"

"For a purpose. There is always a purpose if you look closely."

Lucy thought, why would she do this to herself, just when her life was getting exciting when things were finally happening when she was happy at last?

"Is there a God?"

Speranza paused. "God. That's always an interesting question because God has many names and a different meaning for everyone. The Universe. The Great Spirit. The Creator. The Force. So many names. But does a name really matter? God as you refer to the word, can be the force of life, or faith or love. God can be the voice that speaks inside you, the voice you can trust to tell you the truth. In my humble opinion, I believe God, as you call it, is the power of love. Love in the hands and the hearts of people who care deeply for others. In you and me."

"You're saying God is a verb?"

"Spoken like a true writer," Speranza smiled. "Yes."

"Now what?" Lucy asked.

"You'll see, my dear. Your future is bright and you will discover things about yourself you never knew."

"Will I ever see my husband again? My family or my friends?"

"You can and you will. I will show you how, but first, we have to get there. We have to follow the Road home. After that, all things are possible."

Lucy dried her eyes.

"You can't think about yesterday, Lucy. Regret is a waste of thought. All you can think about now is this moment and all the things you can do with it."

The idea gave Lucy comfort. She guessed the mood swings had to do with the transition, probably the most momentous change there was in life. She took a deep breath and listened to her heart. It told her to relax. The feelings swung from giddiness to despair. How would she get accustomed to this new Reality?

As they walked, Lucy noticed spruce trees that grew buds of confetti lights. They illuminated their path with a colorful glow. Castles and statues of unfamiliar creatures made of sand sparkled in the powdery moonlight. Four little white birds sang a song she knew. Happy Birthday. Now she knew why the song came to her again. It was her birthday. She died on her birthday, Lucy realized. She entered life and left it on the same day. What an extraordinary coincidence, she thought. What did it mean? She had trouble remembering her age.

"How old am I? I mean, how old was I?"

"Thirty-four," answered Speranza, "then. You are any age you want to be now. Pick one you're comfortable with and it's yours."

"Really?" But it didn't matter what age she was. She was the same person, whether she was four or thirty-four or four. It didn't matter. Just BE, she thought. That's what she was doing. Just being.

Lucy looked around and took in the extraordinary sights of this Reality.

"It's so beautiful," whispered Lucy. "I still can't believe I'm dead. Everything seems so real here."

Speranza smiled. "You are finally coming around, my dear." she said, "But you are not dead. You are alive, just in a different way."

She used to think about the possibility of life after death and never knew if it was true. But here she was, alive and well, living in a land beyond her imagination. Was it possible there really was life after life?

She thought about the possibility of invisible things existing beyond her realm of vision. She thought of science and sound waves, facsimiles and cyberspace, atoms and protons, the universe and light years, black holes, and distant galaxies. If all these things existed and more, then why not the reality of life existing beyond the physical? No one knew because no one had yet discovered a way to create communication. Before phones and the internet, no one imagined communicating to distant places without actually being there or sending a letter.

Maybe that was something she could do, find a way to break the invisible barrier between life and death. As Father Mike had told her, there were so many more things to be discovered, things that have no name but exist, waiting to be recognized. That would be her mission here, she decided, to find that knowledge and use it to help people connect with those they left behind. She considered these thoughts and found inspiration. She was still thinking, still creating, as she always did. She was still making new ideas, even after her death.

Golden sun spilled orange light on her face. It was morning and even though she hadn't slept all night, she wasn't tired. She saw something on the horizon.

"We have arrived," said Speranza.

CHAPTER 10

A TENT DRAPED WITH billowing white silk, decorated with string lights and lavender flowers sat on the horizon. The sand was now silvery-white and sparkling, as if it had been mixed with diamond dust. The shimmering substance stuck to her skin and dotted her black pants like glitter. A cool, delicious breeze caressed her face. It reminded her of a warm summer day at the beach. She breathed it in and felt like a part of it, made of it, and at one with it.

The Little Boy stepped out from the tent.

"It's you," Lucy said, amazed. He seemed different to her now, more childlike, less strange.

"Hello, Jude," Speranza addressed the Little Boy. "Good to see you again."

"Jude?" said Lucy.

"I am Possibility," said the Little Boy in his small voice. "I am eternal hope. I am home. I am the purist state of being. But you can call me Jude too. That is what everyone calls me. Follow me," he said. "We are almost ready. Now everyone is here."

"Everyone?" asked Lucy.

"Yes. We were waiting for you."

It all made sense now. She finally understood what the Little Boy was looking for. He was looking for her, for the people who were like her. She understood now . He personified hope. The thing she was looking for, even though she didn't know it at the time she met him. There were so many things she didn't know then, but now, she knew. That wish she had made on a star so long ago as she sat on the cement with Hero. It finally came true for her. Lucy had found her answers. But had Hero found his?

"Have you seen my friend, Hero?" she asked Jude.

"We were not waiting for him," said the Little Boy.

"Be happy for Hero," said Speranza. "You gave him a great gift. I promise you, he is fine and is going back to his home in his Reality. Your friend has a lot more good deeds to accomplish. You will see him again, but not yet."

"Come," said Jude with excitement. "It's almost time."

"Time for what?" asked Lucy.

"Time for the celebration," Speranza said.

They followed Jude toward the tent.

"Is he the same one, you know, as the saint on the card we read in my house?" Lucy whispered to Speranza.

Speranza smiled. "He is Hope. As hopeful as a child. You will soon see how different things are here. You will be surprised, Lucy."

They followed Jude into the tent decorated with colorful lights.

Inside, toys, stuffed animals, and bouquets of flowers lay on the sandy floor. Pictures of smiling people were safety pinned to the silky walls. There were hundreds of faces. She looked at a photo of a young woman in a glamorous pose with long, dark hair and exotic features. Beneath the picture, it read: "She loves

to laugh. Have you heard her wonderful laughter recently? "
That made Lucy smile. She was overwhelmed by a sense of joy.

Lucy and Speranza followed the Little Boy through the tent and out the other side. There they were. All the people. Thousands gathered, from all walks of life, standing in a semicircle, facing the tent. They clapped. Were they waiting for Jude? Were they waiting for her? She assumed they were all dead too, but alive at the same time.

Here she was, in the company of complete strangers. No matter where each of them had come from, what religion they followed, or what they believed, they had one thing in common. They were all here at the same time, experiencing the same moment. They were living in the same Reality.

She checked her pocket and found only sand. Of course, she thought, she had given the leaf to Hero and left the key in the door of the office marked 104. She looked at the sand. It was different from the sand beneath her feet. But yet, it was proof of something. She let it sift through her fingers. It melted into the silvery, sparkling sand below. She couldn't see it anymore. Did it really exist after all? She didn't know. She didn't care. She stood in the moment and took it all in.

Speranza led her to a place in the crowd. None of these people stepped into this moment alone. Each had a personal guide who stood by them, proudly. She was able to tell the difference between the people who were like her and the people who were the guides. Or guardians. There was a difference between those who lived in the flesh and the spirits and those who had never been "born."

She looked at Speranza and saw her differently now. She really did look angelic, unmarred by worry and stress. Her face was bright, with a light that shone from the inside out. She was not like a typical human. She was lighter. Almost made of glass.

Lucy studied the crowd, scanning the faces. She recognized Father Mike. He winked at her. She waved at him. Seeing him made her feel at home. There were people here she knew. This gave her comfort. She was part of a bigger family.

Everyone gathered in a circle. Lucy felt a sense of peace and unity among the group. Thousands of people from different eras and worlds held flickering candles that dotted the landscape. Some were just arriving, while others were veterans of the land. All were there to witness the indoctrination of its new citizens. Who was telling her this? She suspected Speranza telepathically transmitted this information. So, this was how it worked here. Things were different. She let the message flow and closed her eyes. Here she was. Here she is, she thought. She still is.

Bubbles rose from the silvery sand. There was a sense of enchantment in this place, where trees grew in different shapes and everything glowed with colorful lights. The smooth, white silk of the distant tent rippled gently in the wind. Within the center of the circle, created by the crowd, was an inner circle made of small votive candles in glass cups pushed into the sand. Lucy felt lucky to be on the inside of the circle, to have a perfect viewing spot. Within the circle of light sat the Little Boy crossed-legged on the ground with his eyes closed. Glittery sand stuck to his entire body and made him shimmer. What was he thinking about?

"Where are we?"

"Your dream, your own personal Heaven. This is where we are."

"With all these other people?"

"They are part of your Heaven too."

"Oh," said Lucy, feeling the excitement in the air. She was beginning to understand.

The Little Boy stood up in the center of the circle. Everyone clapped.

"Welcome, everyone," he said in a small voice. "Today we are free."

"We are free," repeated the crowd. Lucy didn't repeat it because she didn't know what she was supposed to do.

"We are free," he said again.

The crowd repeated, "We are free. We are free."

"We are free!" Lucy joined in.

"In a few minutes, we will make a connection with the loved ones we left behind. Please, hold hands and focus your thoughts on the ones you love."

Everyone joined hands. Lucy held hands with Speranza and an older gentleman to her right, who gave her a warm smile. The Little Boy they called Jude stood in the center and closed his eyes.

There was silence. Others closed their eyes too. She watched how some smiled to themselves, lost in a memory, while others had their eyes open as if concentrating on a distant sound. She looked at Speranza, who looked back at her with her comforting eyes. It's all right, said a voice in her head. It's all right, she heard again. Everything was right. Everything that had seemed wrong before was now right.

Softly, it began. The silky sound of a single violin filled the air with a bittersweet ballad that tugged at Lucy's heartstrings. The sound was distant as if it were in the back of her head.

Lucy wondered whether she heard it with her ears or her soul and listened as it grew louder, now accompanied by other instruments. The melody, now supported by a symphony, included the angelic voices of a choir. Violins, cellos, piano, and voices swelled, filling the air and Lucy's spirit.

"To those souls in Heaven, we tell you we love you and we are thinking of you," said a man's voice, which seemed to come from below the ground.

Lucy was moved. She felt the connection. Two realities interfaced, but only one reality knew about the other. This moment exaggerated the separation she felt. There was a disconnection between her then and her now. Emotions welled up. The music came to a crescendo. Lucy looked at Little Boy Jude. She saw herself in the reflection of his eyes - she looked radiant and beautiful. She released the tension she held since she arrived. The unknown was not terrifying anymore. The fear was gone. The mystery was revealed. The weight and responsibility of having a human body was over. Lucy felt the difference. She felt like she had just woken up after a good night's sleep. Alive. The scent of flowers. The pink morning light. A joyful moment. Yes, she knew who she was. Yes, she did find hope again, as Father Mike had promised she would. Lucy finally understood. She was free.

CHAPTER 11

FREEDOM HAD NEW MEANING here. The moment Lucy realized her freedom, she had the unique ability to be in two places at once.

Lucy found herself standing in a crowd in New York City, in Battery Park. There weren't enough chairs for the people who arrived to remember those they had lost one bright September day. There were musicians in one corner, under a tree, and a choir of children nearby. Police officers stood guard in several places. A minister stood at the podium in front of the audience. A beautiful fall day. She didn't know what year it was. She breathed in the autumn air and realized she was floating. She couldn't feel her feet touch the ground. She looked around and spotted Frank, sitting in a folding chair, wearing his gray suit, the one she had bought for him a week before her last day. He told her he didn't like it, it wasn't his style, but today, it looked so good on him. The gray, European-cut jacket accentuated his broad, muscular shoulders and the triangle shape of his back. She loved Frank's body, especially his back. She glided to him instantly, as if jet-propelled. It was like riding a bike for the first time. The movement took her by surprise. It was a very different feeling from flesh and bone, where she had to put one foot in front of the other to get somewhere. This was faster, more instantaneous. She stood in front of him. Frank's eyes were puffy and red.

"Frank, can you see me?"

He didn't respond.

"Frankie, can you hear me?"

Frank blinked and looked around. Did he hear her? He moved a strand of hair from his forehead and rubbed his eyes. If he heard her, he didn't acknowledge it. She watched his eyes wander in the sky to look at a cloud. One singed purple cloud resided in the otherwise empty sky. She could hear his thoughts. Convertible. Road trip. Arizona. Lucy and Frank. The cloud brought back a memory from a time when they were dating.

Lucy waved her hands in front of Frank's face. "I'm here, baby. I'm here."

Lucy waited. Did he feel her presence?

He dropped his head and closed his eyes. He wasn't ready. She was, but he wasn't.

She combed her fingers through his thick, curly hair. "I will always love you," she whispered and felt herself melt into the air.

LUCY WAS NOW IN A HOSPITAL corridor, with no idea how she got there. Doctors and nurses rushed through the hallway. Lucy turned a corner and went through a steel green door without having to push or pull. Why was she here? She entered one patient's room. A young man rested behind a curtain. An older man beside him. Lucy glided closer. She recognized the young man. It was Hero. The older man held Hero's hand.

"Kevin, my boy. I know you can hear me. Open your eyes again. Open them again for your dad," the older man whispered. "Come on, I know you can do it again."

"Kevin," Lucy said. "So that's who you are. Kevin. But what's in a name, anyway. Right?"

Lucy stood with the older man. "Hero. Kevin. Listen to your dad and open your eyes."

Kevin stirred and mumbled something in his semi-conscious state. She couldn't understand him. His eyes moved beneath the lids, then popped open. "Pretty One!"

"Can you see me?"

Kevin looked directly at her. Maybe he did.

"Kevin!" his father cried out. "Kevin, my boy. You're awake."

But Kevin didn't look at his father. He kept his eyes on Lucy. She took his hand. Kevin's father yelled for a nurse. He left the room, looking for someone.

Lucy locked her eyes with Kevin's.

He flashed a smile. "Pretty One, are you okay?"

"Yes." She was thrilled he could actually see her.

"I am alive and well," she said and touched his forehead. Maybe because Kevin was in a coma, maybe that's why he could see her.

Kevin's father returned and saw Kevin talking to himself. He thought his son was hallucinating. "Kevin, my son. Kevin, can you see me?"

Kevin looked at his father, who grabbed his hand and cried

Lucy saw a familiar statue on a nearby table. She didn't have to move closer to read the tiny inscription etched into its base: "St. Jude, give us hope." Beneath that, it read, "St. Jude's Hospital." A small blue votive light flickered next to the statue. She realized Hero had not been dreaming when he described this experience. He actually lived it as he teetered between two worlds. He wasn't teetering anymore.

She was able to read his wristband without looking at it: Kevin James McDonald. That was his name. That is his name. Her name was Lucy Casey Smith.

Hero and Pretty One, two generic souls without names or places, were nomads in a world between worlds. They tried hard to find the answers and now they had them.

Kevin's father crossed himself and thanked the St. Jude statue. He told Kevin how lucky it was for a father to find a son in a fire. He talked about the miracle that saved both their lives. Then, Lucy heard him tell Kevin a story.

One of the boys from Ladder Company 9 heard this from someone at the scene. He wasn't sure if it was true. The guy told Kevin's father that Kevin had risked his life in an attempt to save a woman trapped in a fiery stairwell. According to the story, Kevin was the only one who had heard her cries. He unknowingly saved his own life when he carried her to safety. That day, his entire company had been wiped out. He was the only survivor, and rumor had it that the pretty young woman was already dead by the time Kevin reached her. Some thought that it was the young woman's ghost who saved Kevin's life. That was the story going around among the firemen. Some of them just wanted to believe it. Kevin's father wanted to believe it. It was printed in three newspapers and Kevin's father couldn't wait for the opportunity to share the story that had made his son famous.

Lucy listened. She knew. She was the pretty dead woman in the stairwell. Even though she didn't remember, she knew she had saved his life. And now, all the pieces had come together. Everything made sense.

She watched father and son relish in life. Like she once had.

Kevin was regaining consciousness, and as he did, he could no longer see her. Lucy felt herself dissolving into the walls, disappearing like a mist, absorbed by her surroundings.

She was there, even though she wasn't really. Lucy lingered in the hospital air long enough to find out about the strange star-shaped leaf a nurse had found in Kevin's pocket. No one could explain where it had come from. It added to the mysterious story and became the talk of the hospital staff. They believed it was the ghost of the pretty young woman who had put the leaf there. Lucy felt good knowing her time with Hero had really existed. Its proof remained.

Later, Lucy learned that Kevin went on to save many people's lives. She now knew his Purple Genie was really his desire for life. In years to come, she knew that Kevin would find a life partner and bring new life into the world.

Because of her, Kevin would live a long and prosperous life.

She knew something else. Kevin would carry that leaf with him for the rest of his life. Her gift would be his talisman.

THAT NIGHT, LUCY WENT to her home, climbed into bed and lay with Frank, who was asleep. Resting her cheek on his undershirt, she hugged him the way she always did. She felt him breathing. She breathed in rhythm with him. She felt the warmth of his body, the texture of his legs against hers. He didn't flinch or move. He was in a deep sleep. Dreaming of her.

"I will always love you, Frank," she whispered and melted with him.

She knew he would think about that dream often, wondering what made it so real. He would keep that dream his secret forever.

LUCY HAD A NEW POWER. She was able to be anywhere she wanted at any time. It was a natural ability, one she did not have to learn. She seeped through concrete. Became part of the furniture. She was able to see inside things. Hear people's thoughts. She could stand in the same room with thousands of other souls yet not see them. They didn't take space. They were like concepts, she realized. She came to know that death was built upon realms of imagination and dreams. She could do all the things within the scope of her imagination. She could influence a thought, and live in someone's dream. She could exist on a page or guide someone's hands. She liked this Reality. She adapted quickly.

Throughout her existence, she watched those she loved, from the fabric of a chair or the light from a ceiling fixture. She became Frank's pillow when he needed her the most. She rode with Hero on his fire trips. She watched her loved ones evolve through time, and gave them signs to tell them she was around. She wished they could see her and communicate.

Lucy became everything.

LUCY WENT BACK HOME, to her personal Heaven. She stood in the center of the silver sand and watched the sunset, feeling connected to where she was and eventually realized this existence was not a place but a state of being that didn't take up space. She was able to move through any Reality she pleased, even if it was in the past. She grew in knowledge and skills but did not grow old. She listened to her inner Wisdom, who showed her the way. She understood Father Mike's words fully. The kingdom of Heaven was inside her all the while. She and her Heaven were one.

She saw little of Speranza but knew she was there. Lucy's spirit expanded into the details of her world. She remained Lucy for as long as she watched over Frank. She watched him live. He studied psychology and changed his career. He worked compassionately to help others and remained single. Frank knew in his heart Lucy was his kindred spirit. On occasion, he saw her in the garden or in the den, where she sometimes stoked the fireplace. Frank felt her presence.

Lucy watched and waited as Frank grew old and kept her identity until she was reunited with Frank. When Frank came to her, she was his companion in a strange land. She walked with him on the Road to a place beyond life as he knew it and experienced all the new things together. Frank, too, came to understand what Lucy had learned, that the journey was a discovery of his true self.

As measureless time moved forward in uncounted years, Lucy lost her identity as Lucy and became Wisdom.

As Wisdom, she dedicated herself to the spirits of lost souls, living and dead. She became the voice of guidance and spoke clearly. She directed people through hardships and trials.

She gave them answers. She gave them hope. They felt Wisdom but could not identify her.

In the future, her voice would help connect the living with the dead in ways never imagined before.

The Road To Beyond © 2022 Micki Pagano

Don't miss out!

Visit the website below and you can sign up to receive emails whenever Micki Pagano publishes a new book. There's no charge and no obligation.

https://books2read.com/r/B-A-VYVT-PWHAC

BOOKS 2 READ

Connecting independent readers to independent writers.

About the Author

On the morning of September 11th, Micki, a Madison Avenue creative, was living in Manhattan when tragedy struck. Her then boyfriend now husband, ran from the burning building. A survivor. In the aftermath of chaos, she noticed a cloud above the place where the Twin Towers once stood. It lingered for weeks, luminous and heavy. It made her wonder. Maybe it wasn't a cloud at all, but the collective souls of those who lost their lives that day, looking down on us. The image - an indelible memory - inspired the story, The Road To Beyond.

Micki has been telling fantastical stories her entire life, whether crafting fiction, producing films or telling a brand story.

A powerful story will make you feel and wonder. It opens a portal to a heighten reality, a day dream away. A good story, no matter what form it takes, is an experience that connects with your heart. And, becomes part of you.

As a Madison Avenue Creative Director, Micki created award-winning campaigns for Coca Cola, P&G, and many more - all through the power of story. Winner of Cannes Lion, Clio, Addy, Effie and Telly Awards, she is currently Creative Director of Branding Shorts [brandingshorts.com], a content-creation agency she co-founded with her husband, Tony Parente, in 2008.

Micki is an artist, writer, filmmaker and mom. She loves magical realism and compelling stories that take us on a journey beyond reality as we know it.

Stay tuned for more.